John Dough and the Cherub

John Dough and the Cherub

A Whimsical Wonder-Story in which is Described the Marvelous
Creation of John Dough, the Gingerbread Man; his meeting
with the Incubator Baby called Chick the Cherub:
their Adventures in the Isle of Phreex, the
Land of Mifkets, Pirate Island and
Hiland and Loland.

BY
L. FRANK BAUM

FOREWORD BY
J. L. BELL

ILLUSTRATED BY
JOHN R. NEILL

Hungry Tiger Press
San Diego

John Dough and the Cherub

ISBN 1-929527-17-9
ISBN 978-1-929527-17-5

Book and Cover design by David Maxine.
Illustrations by John R. Neill from the original 1906 edition.
Frontispiece by John R. Neill from *The Road to Oz* (1909).

The publisher would like to thank Paul Bienvenue, Marcus Mébès,
Eric Shanower, and Bill Thompson for loaning
materials for reproduction.

John Dough and the Cherub was originally published in 1906 by
The Reilly and Britton Co., of Chicago.

This work of fiction by L. Frank Baum contains a number of
racial and ethnic stereotypes that may be considered offensive today.
The original text is reprinted here in an unabridged and unaltered form
except for corrections of typographical errors and missing punctuation.

HUNGRY TIGER PRESS
**5995 Dandridge Lane, Suite 121
San Diego, CA 92115-6575**

Visit our website at:
www.hungrytigerpress.com

FOREWORD

The tale of *John Dough and the Cherub* began when author L. Frank Baum met with magazine editor Edward Bok, sometime around 1903 or 1904.

Baum was at his height of value as an author. He had written two best-selling children's books, *Father Goose* (1899) and *The Wonderful Wizard of Oz* (1900). The latter had reached an even bigger audience as a theatrical extravaganza. The Bobbs-Merrill Company was issuing a new fantasy novel by Baum each year. In 1904 he began writing a serial for *St. Nicholas,* America's most prestigious magazine for children, and *The Delineator* commissioned his "Animal Fairy Tales." In that same period, Edward Bok contacted Baum about writing for the *Ladies' Home Journal*. As Baum recalled in a 1912 letter to his publisher, "he offered me $2500. for the serial rights of a fairy book."

Bok was younger than Baum by seven years but had been established in publishing longer. Starting in 1889, he had pushed the *Ladies' Home Journal* onto the literary scene with a combination of energy, celebrity, and high standards. Soon it had over a million subscribers, more than any other magazine in the world. Among Bok's editorial strategies was wooing well-known authors for children. He befriended Rudyard Kipling and published some *Just So Stories* in 1902. The next year, Bok commissioned Maxfield Parrish, the rising young artist who had illustrated Baum's first children's book, to create five paintings. The editor's overture to Baum, America's newly famous children's author, was apparently part of that strategy of going after big names.

Children's fairy stories were a departure from Bok's usual material, however. As the name *Ladies' Home Journal* implied, almost all of the magazine's fiction was written for middle-class women and showed women in realistic settings. Each issue offered a still-familiar mix of nonfiction: celebrity profiles, recipes, decorating advice, etiquette rulings, fashion tips, health warnings, and moral exhortations. Bok went beyond domestic tasks to include articles on literature, art, and current events, serving women who were intelligent and curious but had little formal education.

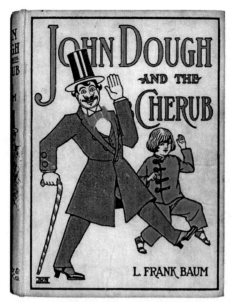

Cover of the First Edition of
John Dough and the Cherub *(1906).*

Even as he chased celebrated authors, however, Bok had a policy "not to commit his magazine to unwritten material, or to accept and print articles or stories simply because they were the work of well-known persons." The *Journal's* circulation meant he could pay more than other editors and ask even bestselling authors to write on speculation. So Baum began creating his new "fairy book" on those terms.

Baum's big successes came from mixing contemporary American details and attitudes into the traditional forms of nursery rhymes and fairy tales. *The Wonderful Wizard of Oz* was, he wrote, "a modernized fairy tale." He brought magic up to date: in *Queen Zixi of Ix* (1905), a witch offers lessons in "the most modern and approved methods." The first paragraph of *John Dough* reflected how it, too, would offer a new take on the traditional as it quotes a bakery's paradoxical promotion: "Home-made Bread by the Best Modern Machinery."

The story Baum set out to modernize is the folk tale now classified by scholars as Aarne-Thompson 2025, "The Runaway Pancake." Variations have been collected in Ireland, Holland, Norway, Russia, and Slovenia. The earliest printed version, "*Von dicken fetten Pfannekuchen* (The Thick, Fat Pancake)," appeared in German in 1854. Robert Chambers put two variants of "The Wee Bunnock" into the 1870 edition of *Popular Rhymes of Scotland,* and in 1889 the *Journal of American Folk-Lore* recorded a version called "Johnny-Cake." But most Americans have heard variations that descend from a story published in *St. Nicholas* in 1875: "The Gingerbread Boy."

In all these stories, a pancake or other baked good unexpectedly rolls or runs away—usually with no clear explanation why or how. It escapes several pursuers with increasing glee but eventually gets eaten, usually by a fox. In some versions the fox simply snaps up the pancake; in others, the animal tricks the runaway into coming too close. By turning the round pancake into boy-shaped gingerbread, the *St. Nicholas* version took the first step toward humanizing the runaway.

Baum went further, naming the gingerbread man and thus making him an individual with novel potential. The name Baum chose reflected his love of puns. Since the seventeenth century British law manuals had used "John Doe" to designate a generic party in a lawsuit. Baum kneaded the surname into "Dough," but his John still strives to be an everyman. A full-sized gingerbread man cannot blend into society, however, because he is too appetizing. Thus, the basic plot of *John Dough* is the same as in "The Runaway Pancake": the baked good flees for his life from one hungry group after another.

Traditional versions of the story take place in rural settings. Baum began his "modernized" tale in an American city. In most of his early fantasy novels, including *Wizard, Dot and Tot in Merryland* (1901), and *The Enchanted Island of Yew* (1903), Baum drew a sharp divide between fairy-lands and the "civilized" world of his readers, where magic no longer belongs. He set the most magical episodes in *The Life and Adventures of*

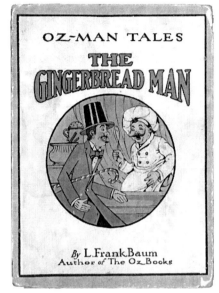

The Gingerbread Man (1917) *reprinted the first four chapters of John Dough.*

Santa Claus (1902) in the distant past. In contrast, the first chapters of *John Dough* take place in the America that *Ladies' Home Journal* readers knew, with shops, streets, and women sweeping their walks. But that America also contains the magical Elixir of Life.

The start of John Dough thus fits into the part of Baum's output that I call "urban fairy tales." Other examples from the same period are the *Queer Visitors from the Marvelous Land of Oz* comic pages (1904-05) and *The Woggle-Bug Book* (1905). But of all Baum's writing, the first four chapters of *John Dough* are most like stories he wrote for newspapers and then collected in *American Fairy Tales* (1901). The novel's start involves a one-drop rheumatism cure, as in "The Glass Dog" from that collection. John Dough resembles "The Dummy That Lived," a figure from a shop-window display who comes to life. (Baum was an expert in store displays, having edited the trade magazine *The Show Window.*)

Baum's urban fairy tales are peopled with the ethnic caricatures that pervaded American popular culture at the time, particularly on stages and comic pages. The 1902 *Wizard* extravaganza, for example, featured a "Ball of All Nations" with slots for songs in Irish, Italian, American Indian, and "Cockney Coon" styles. *American Fairy Tales* includes Italian robbers and Irish policemen. Probably the height—or depth—of Baum's ethnic caricaturing appeared in *The Woggle-bug Book*, which Reilly & Britton insisted "will be enjoyed by every one—men, women and children" (as described by an ad in early copies of *John Dough*). Baum usually sidestepped such depictions in his children's books, but apparently felt that adults wanted this sort of humor.

Most of the characters we meet in the first chapters of *John Dough* are ethnic types. The Grograndes, who name means "fat-big" in poor French, are bakers from Paris. (That adds irony to Madame Tina's worry about being "killed by a lot of desperate foreigners.") Ali Dubh and his pursuers are even more exotic: "although their forms were muffled in long cloaks, the turbans they wore and the glint of their dark, beady eyes proclaimed them children of the desert." Baum repeatedly emphasizes how Ali Dubh can "steal softly away." This stereotype of Arabs — immediately identifiable yet moving undetected through our cities, hot-tempered and violent — survives in today's warnings about ubiquitous Islamist "sleeper cells." Though John Dough may not represent any particular ethnicity, he is a sort of immigrant as well, a newcomer who struggles to fit in and worries about being eaten alive. This multiethnic cast comes together on America's national holiday, the Fourth of July.

No manuscript of *John Dough* survives, so it is impossible to say for sure what Baum sent to Bok. But I suspect he submitted only those first four chapters as a sample. Their combined word count equals the length of two serial installments for the *Journal*, enough for Bok to make up his mind. Those installments would explain John Dough's origin, provide a complete episode in his flight through the city, and end with an explosive cliffhanger to make the magazine's readers eager for more.

In The Road to Oz, *Neill included characters from* John Dough *in his endpaper illustrations. Counterclockwise from the left, this image shows Ali Dubh, Jules Grogrande, Para Bruin, Pittypat the rabbit, (whom Baum described as small, but Neill consistently drew as large as a child), John Dough, Chick the Cherub, and a Mifket. (At bottom are a Winged Monkey and the Wicked Witch of the West.)*

But Bok declined the manuscript. In 1912 Baum summed up the editor's response: "He refused the story unless I would write in a child character, and I either had a grouch or the big-head and refused to alter the text." The rejection seemed to sting, even many years later, since Baum repeated "that Mr. Bok himself proposed the serialization." The editor had come to him, a star author, but then demanded he change his work.

In fact, Bok was right. The first chapters of *John Dough* offer magic and action, but no sympathetic child—only Ned Robbins with his slang, firecrackers, and sweet tooth. The most prominent character in the two opening chapters is Madame Tina, a middle-aged woman. Whether or not he set out to do it, Baum had written for the women who read the *Ladies' Home Journal*, not for their children.

In time, Baum realized the value of Bok's advice. As he told Sumner Britton in 1912, "I thought better of his criticism, however, and later wrote in the Cherub and gave the book to you." Britton had partnered with Frank Reilly in 1904 to publish *The Marvelous Land of Oz*, Baum's follow-up to *Wizard*. Sometime in the following months Baum sold Reilly & Britton the story he called *John Dough, the Baker's Man*, not telling them that one of America's leading editors had rejected it.

In October 1905, Baum tied his career even more closely to Reilly & Britton with a comprehensive contract. In essence, he chose to be the big frog in their small pond: a little publisher's most important author rather than one of many authors at a larger firm. He agreed to supply many books under several names. Reilly & Britton committed to publish no book for children in 1906 except *John Dough* without Baum's permission. They also promised to promote that and all his subsequent titles "to the full extent of whatever ability God had given them."

Reilly & Britton had contracted with the young Philadelphian John R. Neill to illustrate *Land*, and they returned to him for *John Dough*. Indeed, from then on no other artist would illustrate the first edition of a Baum fantasy novel for children. Neill's art in *Land* was a mix of line drawings and color plates. Reilly & Britton chose a different design for *John Dough*, with no plates on expensive paper. Instead, the endpapers, frontmatter, full-page illustrations, and chapter openers were printed in three colors: black, red, and either blue, green, or yellow in different signatures. All other drawings were printed in black. Neill drew additional illustrations for the newspapers that syndicated *John Dough*, such as the *Minneapolis Sunday Tribune* and *Washington Star*.

When Baum went back to *John Dough*, determined to leave the *Ladies' Home Journal* behind, he wrote in a new rhythm. His first four chapters had averaged fewer than 1,800 words each. The fifth chapter stretches to 6,800, almost as many as the first four together. That chapter also lifts the story out of Edward Bok's America to the fantastic island of Phreex. In a sense, Baum restarted his story on his own terms.

The fifth chapter introduces the child that Bok had recommended. Chick the Cherub seizes John's "soft brown hand," and seizes control. It is impossible to imagine the rest of the novel without this Incubator Baby. (That fact is the strongest evidence that Baum did not send Bok a complete version of the story. Baum was not a diligent rewriter, and if he had had a full manuscript without a child he would have sold it to Reilly & Britton.) By the time *John Dough and the Cherub* was published, Chick had sauntered all the way up into its title and was the focus of its marketing campaign—"dominating an entire book," in the words of a publicity article.

Cute, blond, and audacious, Chick is an ideal. Almost too ideal, in fact. As a fictional character, the Cherub is too cheerful to require reader sympathy. Chick has only one worry: indigestion from eating something besides oatmeal and cream. Fortunately for John, the Incubator Baby's digestive frailty dovetails with his own biggest fear—being eaten. He can accept Chick as a companion with no worry about the child eating gingerbread, just as later he can feel safe around Para Bruin, the rubber bear who never eats at all.

The Cherub is most appealing as a foil for John. The gingerbread man is anxiously cautious; the child is happy and confident. John is full of ancient wisdom, but lacks Chick's knowledge of the modern world. The Incubator Baby is outspoken and uses the latest slang; John has old-fashioned manners. "You have a queer way of expressing yourself, my friend," John tells Chick. The child sweetly replies, "you always know what I mean, don't you? . . . Then don't kick." In this pairing of a child with a newly created artificial person, Baum recreated the dynamics of Dorothy and the Scarecrow in *Wizard* and Tip and Jack Pumpkinhead in *Land*. All these couples upend the usual relationship of children and adults. The bigger partner is the naïf, making the child into the wise leader—a situation to delight young readers.

But in a very important way, the Cherub is unlike Dorothy or Tip. This "modernized" tale never labels Chick as a girl or a boy. Baum had explored the theme of gender switching in previous books. In *Yew* a female fairy turns into an adventurous young knight named Prince Marvel. The mischievous boy Tip whom readers meet in the first paragraph of *Land* turns out to be dainty princess Ozma under enchantment; that revelation has startled more than a few young readers. But Chick presents the biggest challenge to our ideas of gender. Prince Marvel and Tip display the standard traits of boys while the fairy and Ozma are quite feminine because those male and female identities are in different bodies, magically exchanged. Chick, however, occupies a place between the two genders.

Scientists debate how much of our conception of feminine or masculine behavior is based on biological factors such as genes and hormones, and how much is based on culture—upbringing, media images, and the like. In this divide between nature and nurture, Baum comes down on the side of nurture. Indeed, he implies that nurture is the *only* thing that produces different expectations for each sex. Not having been raised by a mother and father, Chick feels no need to identify as girl or boy. The Incubator Baby is as genderless as the incubator itself. Baum, an expert on raising Hamburg chickens, knew the name "Chick" was doubly appropriate for this child: chicks had been hatched in incubators for years, and chicks are notoriously difficult to sex.

Through careful writing, Baum left Reilly & Britton with a question they would use to **promote** *John Dough:* is the Cherub a boy or a girl? Baum's *Queer Visitors* **comic** pages had already challenged newspaper readers to answer the **weekly** question, "What did the Woggle-bug say?" The promotion strategy **may** also have been influenced by the puzzle in every issue of the *Ladies' Home Journal;* readers had to submit answers on the designated page of the **magazine**, ensuring that they bought copies. Similarly, early printings of *John Dough* invited young readers to send in their 25-word answers about Chick on the special form bound inside the book. The back cover teased, "The Great John Dough Mystery."

The Great John Dough Mystery
Is the Cherub a Girl or a Boy?

Chick as a Boy   The Cherub of the Story   Chick as a Girl

So that the children who are reading Mr. Baum's delightful·story, "John Dough and the Cherub," can get an idea of how Chick the Cherub would look dressed as a boy and as a girl, we induced the artist, Mr. Neill, to make these pictures. It will be interesting to compare them with the illustrations printed with each installment of the story.

"The Great John Dough Mystery" actually involved Chick the Cherub: was the Incubator Baby a girl or a boy? To promote the contest in newspapers, John R. Neill drew pictures of Chick dressed in fashionable male and female clothing as well as the Cherub's usual garb of pajamas and sandals.

On Phreex, however, no one cares about Chick's gender. Most folks are wrapped up in themselves or their own interests. The island seems to have three groups of inhabitants, starting with the sorts of freaks displayed at circuses and fairs: the fat lady! the two-headed dog! the prize potato! In this group, the live wooden Indian and the general who has been replaced limb for limb, like the Tin Woodman, surpass even what the Ringling Brothers could show.

Chick fits in with these curiosities because in the early 1900s incubator babies were on public display. Machines keeping premature newborns warm were located not in hospitals (in 1900 less than ten percent of American mothers gave birth there), but in exhibit halls at places like Coney Island, the 1901 Pan-American Exposition in Buffalo, and the 1904 Louisiana Purchase Exposition in St. Louis. Such displays spread the news of this technology—and brought in money to pay for it. No matter how cute, Chick is as much of a freak as the two-legged horse.

The second group of Phreex islanders consists of inventors, scientists, and avant-garde artists, recalling the natural philosophers on Laputa in the third leg of *Gulliver's Travels*. While some of these men insist that "no one who succeeds has a right to live in the Isle of Phreex," many have achieved feats well ahead of American scientists in 1906, or even now. Sir Pryse Bocks can repel gravity, though his device needs a more reliable power source. The engineer under the castle makes diamonds so well that he has destroyed the local market for them. Imar's flying-machine exactly replicates a bird's musculature—and appeared in print two years before the Wright brothers made the first official public demonstration of their airplane.

Chick fits in with the inventors as well as the freaks because an Incubator Baby represented the latest in obstetric science. The first description of a machine to preserve premature babies appeared in France in 1857, but the technology improved and expanded in the 1890s. The American press discussed incubators avidly, and in November 1904 Bok's competitor *Good Housekeeping* started to serialize Ellis Parker Butler's humorous novel *The Incubator Baby*. Writers discussed the technology the way later generations reported on "test tube babies," prenatal surgery, and gene therapy: no one begrudged the families who benefited, yet the way science was changing childbirth produced deep worries. Today, of course, a baby who spends time in an incubator is no more remarkable than any other.

The third group on Phreex consists of thoroughly disagreeable and useless sorts, starting with the Brotherhood of Failings. Not even at a freak show would a person want to run into such schlemiels. Unfortunately, the island's absolute ruler comes from this segment of the population. Phreex's kinglet is, in fact, a rare figure in Baum's writings: a brat. He is "nothing more than a spoilt child," as *Baum's Juvenile Speaker* would later sum him up. The kinglet's habit of condemning subjects to death provides a little drama in these chapters, but overall Baum seems to have been killing time until Ali Dubh puts John on the run again, this time with Chick as a companion.

Read This Before You Read the Book

The Great
JOHN DOUGH MYSTERY
Is the Cherub Girl or Boy?
$500.00 for the Best Answers

The Owner of this Book if not Over 16 Years Old is Eligible to Compete

The publishers of John Dough and the Cherub are in doubt as to whether the Cherub is a girl or a boy. The author, Mr. L. Frank Baum, may know, but if so, he has not told us. We have, therefore, determined to allow Mr. Baum's little friends to decide the question, and offer $500.00, divided into 135 gifts, for the best solutions of the mystery.

Chick, the Cherub, is one of the two most important personages in the story and the character is complex and many-sided. Some of Chick's traits seem to indicate that he is a boy, while others point to her being a girl. Some of the expressions Chick uses lean one way and some another. But read for yourself and send in your answers and reasons.

HOW THE GIFTS WILL BE AWARDED

A committee consisting of Mr. Baum, Mr. Henry M. Hyde, author and editor, and Mr. Wilbur D. Nesbit, of the Chicago Evening Post, will select from the answers received the 135 which give the **best reasons** for the conclusion that Chick is a boy or is a girl; the majority of these will determine the answer as to the first question. The gifts will be awarded to the 135 children in the order of the excellence of the reasons given. Awards will be made and the gifts distributed on or before January 15th, 1907, as follows:

LIST OF GIFTS

1	gift of	.	.	.	.	.	.	.	$100.00
1	" "	.	.	.	.	.	.	.	50.00
2	" " $25.00	.	.	.	.	.	.	.	50.00
9	" " 10.00	.	.	.	.	.	.	.	90.00
22	" " 5.00	.	.	.	.	.	.	.	110.00
100	" " 1.00	.	.	.	.	.	.	.	100.00
									$500.00

To Question No. 1, the answer must be but one word—Boy or Girl.

To Question No. 2, the answer must not contain more than 25 words, but as many less as desired.

Only children not over 16 years old may compete. The blank below must be used in competing. Fill in the blank and mail before January 1st, 1907, to

THE REILLY & BRITTON CO., PUBLISHERS, CHICAGO

NOTE—The above offer expires December 31st, 1906. Answers not written on blanks from books, and not mailed before January 1st, 1907, as shown by postmark on envelope, will not be considered.

Tear off the blank here
- -

THESE ARE THE QUESTIONS

1. Is Chick a Boy or a Girl? ANSWER_____

2. Why do you think so? ANSWER (in not over 25 words)_____ _____

_____
_____
_____
_____

My name is_____ I live in_____

At (street address)_____

State of_____ and am_____ years of age.

Mail this slip before December 31st, 1906, with your answers plainly written in ink, to
THE REILLY & BRITTON CO., DEXTER BUILDING, CHICAGO

Early printings of John Dough and the Cherub *contained a form inviting young readers to enter a contest by writing why they felt Chick was a boy or a girl. According to the author's son Frank Joslyn Baum, Reilly & Britton awarded $100 first prizes to two children: one who said Chick was female, and one who said male.*

Over most of the novel, as the gingerbread man and the Cherub fly from one hostile island to another, they move backward in civilization. With its cadre of inventors and flashing electric signs, Phreex is a futuristic society. In contrast, the next island has an antique air, which Neill emphasizes by dressing its ladies and gentlemen in medieval style. There in the Palace of Romance, Chick and John must tell an interesting story night after night or die, a plight Baum borrowed from the tale of Scheherazade, set down in the 1300s.

Leaving Romance behind, John and Chick go further back in civilization to the island of the Mifket, a missing-link "creature that is neither an animal nor a man." Baum makes the Mifket's place on the chain of being even clearer in *Rinkitink in Oz*, which presents one as a stage in transforming a goat back into a human—higher than "a lower form of a man" but not fully human. The Mifkets' king says, "the Arabs are probably descended from our race," and the implication that Ali Dubh is also a lower form of human exposes the racism that could infect Baum's use of ethnic types.

John and Chick complete their backwards journey on the Mifkets' island when they enter the fairy beaver domain, even more ancient than the society of primitive manikins outside. In the traditional gingerbread-boy story, the runaway is chased and eventually eaten by animals. John, in contrast, receives help from the animals because he knows all their languages. Para Bruin, the bouncing bear, becomes a particularly good friend; like the Cowardly Lion, this fearsome-looking beast is actually harmless and lovable. The Fairy Beaver King is the first humane ruler John meets. The Phreex kinglet's rulings were tyrannical, the Palace of Romance's law cruel, the Mifket customs violent—but animals offer John safety and justice.

The chapters on the Mifkets' island form the most substantial and exciting episode of the book. John discovers (perhaps at the same time that Baum decided it) that the Elixir has not only brought him to life, but also given him superhuman strength. Ali Dubh catches up with John again for a final confrontation. The gingerbread man's climactic escape to the fairy beavers is a complex series of events involving birds and rabbits, Para and the Arab, the Mifkets and the human castaways. All in all, it is a satisfying fairy-tale adventure.

At a deeper level, these chapters also show John maturing and becoming worthy of his powers. He faces his existential fear of being eaten as a Mifket bites off one finger, then another. Earlier, John has focused on saving himself. On the island of the Mifkets, he learns to give up a bit of himself, literally, to help a friend. The little girl he saves, Princess Jacquelin, is another unusual type of child for Baum, though common in Victorian literature: the dying child. As usual, it's not clear what the child is dying of—but she's clearly dying. By letting the Princess eat what's left of his left hand, John restores her to health. Then he and Chick help to restore her to her parents. John and his friends still need the advice and magic of the Fairy Beaver King, but this gingerbread man has shown that he deserves that aid.

At this point in his novel, Baum's creativity seems to falter. Like Chick desperately seeking more adventures for the astonishing Silver Pig, the author appears to flail about for inspiration. It looks to me as if Baum fell back on thinking about what might work on stage. With most of his income coming from the *Wizard* extravaganza, Baum could not have helped musing on the dramatic possibilities of his stories.

Some theatrical conventions appear in *John Dough* from the start. John is a fine role for a comedian, and Para Bruin one for an animal impersonator. In the early 1900s many pretty young actresses specialized in "trouser roles" as boys or young men, so the ambiguously gendered Chick would have been easy to cast. (Indeed, when Baum commissioned a silent-movie adaptation of *John Dough* in 1908, Chick was played by actress Grace Elder. The role of John went to comedian Joseph Schrode, who was also an animal impersonator.) Theatrical magic might even have inspired some episodes of the novel. In one showstopper from the *Wizard* extravaganza, the Scarecrow was taken apart piece by piece and reassembled across the stage; the Fairy Beaver King uses the same trick to sneak John up to Para's cave.

Too often when Baum borrowed something popular from the stage, however, he did not add enough to make the results dramatic. Pirates had been a hit in J. M. Barrie's play *Peter Pan*, so Baum took John to "Pirate Island"—where nothing much happens. In late 1905 the *Wizard* stage show was retooled with a slapstick routine called "Football," in which the Scarecrow's head got mixed up with the ball. Around the same time Baum apparently created Sport, whose "head was a foot-ball." But Sport has even less to do than the pirates. The visit to Pirate Island removes the diamonds pressed into John's chest back on Phreex, but otherwise it could have been dug out of the book with no loss.

None too soon, John, Chick, and Para Bruin (conveniently if inexplicably freed from the language barrier) arrive on the island of Hiland and Loland. As with Oz, Merryland, and Yew, this Baum fairyland is strictly divided into different regions and nations. The tall, thin Hilanders look down on the short, round Lolanders, and the citizens cannot even agree on the name of their capitol. While the laws of this island are just as foolish as on the others, this time they benefit the new arrivals. The two nations share a legend that they will receive a "wise

The character of Sport, who has a football for a head, might have been inspired by the success of "Football," a number added to the stage musical of The Wizard of Oz *in late 1905. As publicity photographs of that routine show, the football resembled the head of the Scarecrow, played by comedian Fred Stone, and hilarity ensued.*

and just ruler who is neither flesh nor blood." At last John has found people who will respect his unusual physical makeup, who will appreciate his judgment rather than his taste. Chick quickly proclaims John king and takes the even more impressive title of Head Booleywag.

Baum ended most of his fantasy novels in this period by saying that they had taken place long ago. *Zixi* tells us how its young protagonists have matured and married, and the final chapters of *Yew* and *Santa Claus* are set long after those books' most magical actions. The last sentences of *John Dough* follow that model, telling us that Chick "grew up" so long ago that records about the Head Booleywag are spotty. Baum had moved *John Dough* far from the America of his first chapters.

Baum did not leave his heroes in that misty past, however. Of all of Baum's fantasy novels, *John Dough* was the easiest to cross-market with the Oz series: it was published by the same firm, illustrated by the same artist. With his typical disregard for consistency, Baum simply made Chick a child again when he had the rulers of Hiland and Loland visit the Emerald City in *The Road to Oz*. Later, a map in *Tik-Tok of Oz* showed John's realm on the same continent as Oz, not on an island after all. From then on, the story of *John Dough* was anchored within the Oz universe.

In 1949, with John Dough *out of print for years and deadlines looming, Jack Snow borrowed the Fairy Beaver King as an important character in* The Shaggy Man of Oz. *He also adapted Baum's Palace of Romance into the Valley of Romance, where the lords and ladies stage theatrical melodramas rather than tell stories.*

In some ways, this novel did lead into the Oz books that Baum would concentrate on for most of his later career. The Fairy Beaver King's Observation Room is a forerunner of the magic picture in *Ozma of Oz*, and his bejeweled underground palace resembles the Nome King's. *John Dough and the Cherub* is more than a third-rate Oz book however. It is unique among Baum's novels in having an artificial person as the protagonist rather than as a supporting character. Furthermore, that hero faces dangers more frightening and final than Baum's usual fare: John Dough's edible body means that he risks obliteration wherever he runs. But in this fairy book, for once, the gingerbread man lives happily ever after.

—J. L. BELL

SOURCES BEYOND BAUM

"A Literary Puzzle for the Children," "The Great John Dough Mystery," and "Contract with Reilly & Britton." reproduced in *The Best of the Baum Bugle, 1967-1969*. Kinderhook, Ill.: International Wizard of Oz Club, 1993.

Ashliman, D. L., webmaster. "The Runaway Pancake," Folklore and Mythology Electronic Texts, www.pitt.edu/~dash/folktexts.html.

Bergen, Fanny D. "English Folk-Tales in America, II: Johnny-Cake." *Journal of American Folk-Lore*, 2 (1889), 60-3.

Bok, Edward. *The Americanization of Edward Bok: The Autobiography of a Dutch Boy Fifty Years After*. New York: Charles Scribner's Sons, 1921.

Butler, Ellis Parker. *The Incubator Baby*. New York: Funk & Wagnalls, 1906.

Chambers, Robert. *Popular Rhymes of Scotland*. 2nd edition. London: W. & R. Chambers, 1870.

Duncan, Ray, webmaster. "Classic Resources in Neonatal-Perinatal Medicine," Neonatology.org.

"For Very Little Folks: The Gin-ger-bread Boy." *St. Nicholas*, May 1875, 448-9.

Gardner, Martin. "Introduction" to *John Dough and the Cherub*. New York: Dover, 1974.

Greene, David L. "The Writing of Two L. Frank Baum Fantasies." *The Baum Bugle*, Autumn 1971, 14-6.

Greene, David L., and Dick Martin. *The Oz Scrapbook*. New York: Random House, 1977.

Hearn, Michael Patrick. *The Annotated Wizard of Oz: Centennial Edition*. New York: W. W. Norton, 2000.

Heiner, Heidi Ann, webmaster. "The Annotated Gingerbread Man," SurLaLuneFairyTales.com.

Jacobs, Joseph, editor. *English Fairy Tales*. New York: G. P. Putnam's Sons, 1890.

– *More English Fairy Tales*. New York: G. P. Putnam's Sons, 1894.

Maund, Patrick. "Bibliographia Baumiana: *John Dough and the Cherub* (1906)." *The Baum Bugle*, Winter 1993, 15-8, 28.

Maxine, David. "Introduction and Notes" to *The Wizard of Oz: Vintage Recordings from the 1903 Broadway Musical*. San Diego: Hungry Tiger Press, 2003.

Rogers, Katharine M. *L. Frank Baum: Creator of Oz*. New York: St. Martin's, 2002.

Swartz, Mark Evan. *Oz before the Rainbow: L. Frank Baum's* The Wonderful Wizard of Oz *on Stage and Screen to 1939*. Baltimore: Johns Hopkins University Press, 2002.

As with all my thinking about Baum and the Oz books, I am grateful for the discussions on the Ozzy Digest/Nonestica, Regalia, and Tik-Tok-Talk email lists.

J. L. Bell is a writer and editor living in Massachusetts. He joined the International Wizard of Oz Club thirty years ago, in elementary school, and is now the editor of *Oziana*, the club's creative magazine. He has written articles and reviews for *The Baum Bugle*, and award-winning fiction for *Oziana* and the fifth issue of *Oz-Story*. A graduate of the Humanities Program at Yale College, Bell also specializes in research and writing on the start of the American Revolution.

A FEW WORDS ON THIS EDITION

In creating this new edition of *John Dough and the Cherub* I strove to make it as close as possible to the original 1906 first edition published by The Reilly and Britton Co. of Chicago. However, it is probably not fair to call this new edition a "facsimile" in that the economics of printing prevented Hungry Tiger Press from issuing the book in color as the first edition was issued. As this project progressed it became clear that other, more subtle changes would have to be made for this new edition as well.

A first edition, first state copy of *John Dough and the Cherub* was scanned for use in this new edition. At that point I realized for the first time how poor the original 1906 printing and production of the book actually were.

The 1906 engraver who prepared the illustrations left a great deal of excess material in the non-image areas of the engravings, resulting in unusual edges, splotches, mysterious lines, and printing scum. After the initial engravings were made from illustrator John R. Neill's artwork, the engraver would normally have done a great deal of handtooling and finishing to the metal plates, such as beveling the edges and routing away unwanted metal from non-image areas of the zinc plates. This process was very poorly executed for *John Dough*. Some of Neill's penciled construction lines, measurement marks, notes to the printer, etc. were also left in the printed book, instead of being erased or eliminated as they should have been. The color is often badly out of register, too. Sometimes the dot patterns spill over into areas where they should not have been placed. Some of the illustrations are positioned crookedly on the pages. Many of these defects have been silently corrected for this new edition. Also, the illustration on page 143 of the first edition has been moved in this new edition to page 141 where it more accurately serves the story.

The illustrations were not the only component of the book to suffer. There was a fair amount of broken and dirty type, and even more oddly, missing punctuation. I discovered one last item of interest in the final stages of preparing this reprint. Reilly and Britton seems to have disliked some of Chick's slang and presumably "corrected" it without Baum's approval. On page 148 of first state copies, Chick says, "'Then don't complain,' said the Baby, sweetly; and the gingerbread man looked at his feet with a puzzled expression . . . ." Baum seems to have noticed this "correction" very quickly and in second state copies of the book it has been restored to, "'Then don't kick,' said the Baby . . . ." Since John Dough looks at his feet in a puzzled manner, clearly "kick" was what Baum originally wrote. Thus this is a previously unknown point identifying the earliest copies of *John Dough and the Cherub*. The text in the Hungry Tiger Press edition has been changed to what I conclude was Baum's original language.

— DAVID MAXINE
HUNGRY TIGER PRESS

John R. Neill's original pictorial endpapers for the first edition of *John Dough and the Cherub*.

John Dough and the Cherub

and the

by

L. Frank Baum

AUTHOR OF
THE WIZARD OF OZ
THE LAND OF OZ
THE WOGGLE-BUG BOOK
FATHER GOOSE
QUEEN ZIXI OF IX
THE ENCHANTED ISLAND
OF YEW, ETC.

ILLUSTRATED BY
John R. Neill

CHICAGO
THE REILLY & BRITTON COMPANY
PUBLISHERS

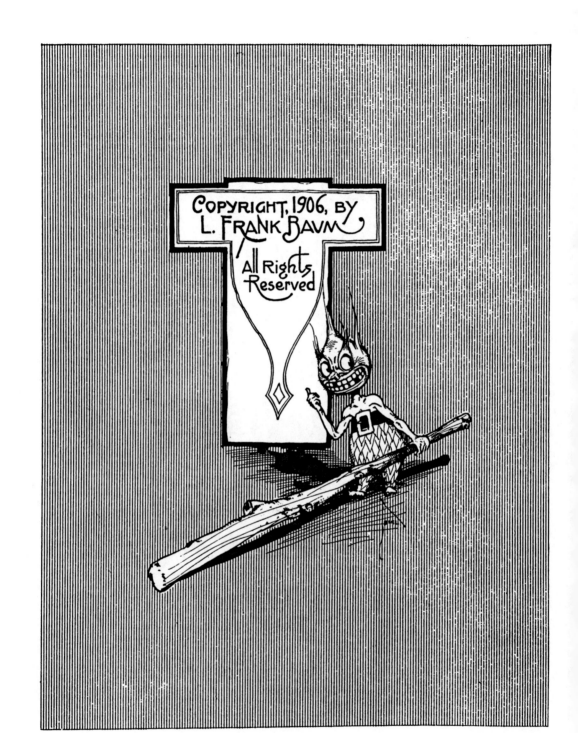

To my young friend
John Randolph Reilly
this book is
affectionately dedicated

LIST OF CHAPTERS

BOY OR GIRL?

The Great Elixir

Over the door appeared a weather-worn sign that read: "JULES GROGRANDE, BAKER." In one of the windows, painted upon a sheet of cardboard, was another sign: "Home-made Bread by the Best Modern Machinery." There was a third sign in the window beyond the doorway, and this was marked upon a bit of wrapping-paper, and said: "Fresh Gingerbread Every Day."

When you opened the door, the top of it struck a brass bell suspended from the ceiling and made it tinkle merrily. Hearing the sound, Madame Leontine Grogrande would come from her little room back of the shop and stand behind the counter and ask you what you would like to purchase.

Madame Leontine—or Madame Tina, as the children called her—was quite short and quite fat; and she had a round, pleasant face that was good to look upon. She moved somewhat slowly, for the rheumatism troubled her more or less; but no one minded if Madame was a bit slow in tying up her parcels. For surely no cakes or buns in all the

9

town were so delicious or fresh as those she sold, and she had a way of giving the biggest cakes to the smallest girls and boys who came into her shop, that proved she was fond of children and had a generous heart.

People loved to come to the Grogrande Bakery. When one opened the door an exquisite fragrance of newly baked bread and cakes greeted the nostrils; and, if you were not hungry when you entered, you were sure to become so when you examined and smelled the delicious pies and doughnuts and gingerbread and buns with which the shelves and show-cases were stocked. There were trays of French candies, too; and because all the goods were fresh and wholesome the bakery was well patronized and did a thriving business.

The reason no one saw Monsieur Jules in the shop was because his time was always occupied in the bakery in the rear—a long, low room filled with ovens and tables covered with pots and pans and dishes (which the skillful baker used for mixing and stirring) and long shelves bearing sugars and spices and baking-powders and sweet-smelling extracts that made his wares taste so sweet and agreeable.

The bake-room was three times as big as the

AN ARAB DASHED INTO THE ROOM.

shop; but Monsieur Jules needed all the space in the preparation of the great variety of goods required by his patrons, and he prided himself on the fact that his edibles were fresh-made each day. In order to have the bread and rolls ready at breakfast time he was obliged to get up at three o'clock every morning, and so he went to bed about sundown.

On a certain forenoon the door of the shop opened so abruptly that the little brass bell made a furious jingling.

An Arab dashed into the room, stopped short, looked around with a bewildered air, and then rushed away again and banged the door after him.

Madame looked surprised, but said nothing. She recognized the Arab to be a certain Ali Dubh, living in the neighborhood, who was accustomed to purchase a loaf from her every morning. Perhaps he had forgotten his money, Madame thought.

When the afternoon was half over he entered again, running as if fiends were at his heels. In the center of the room he paused, slapped his forehead despairingly with both palms, and said in a wailing voice:

"They're after me!"

Next moment he dashed away at full speed, even

forgetting to close the door; so Madame came from behind the counter and did it herself. She delayed a moment to gaze at the figure of Ali Dubh racing up the street. Then he turned the corner of an alley and disappeared from view.

Things did not startle Madame easily; but the Arab's queer behavior aroused in her a mild curiosity, and while she stood looking through the glass of the door, and wondering what had excited the man, she saw two strange forms glide

past her shop with a stealthy motion and proceed in the same direction Ali Dubh had taken.

They were also Arabs, without a doubt; for although their forms were muffled in long cloaks, the turbans they wore and the glint of their dark, beady eyes proclaimed them children of the desert.

When they came to the alley where Ali Dubh had disappeared, the two strangers were joined by a third, who crept up to them with the sly, cat-like tread Madame had noted, and seemed to confer with them. Afterward one turned to the east, a second continued up the street, and the third stole into the alley.

"Yes," thought Madame, "they are after Ali Dubh, sure enough. But if they move so slowly they are not likely to catch the poor fellow at all."

Now, Madame knew very little of her queer customer; for although he made a daily visit to the bakery for a loaf and a few cakes, he was of a gloomy disposition, and never stopped for a chat or a bit of gossip. It was his custom to silently make his simple purchases and then steal softly away.

Therefore his excited actions upon this eventful day were really remarkable, and the good lady was puzzled how to explain them.

She sat late in the shop that evening, burning a

dingy oil lamp that swung in the center of the
room. For her rheumatism was more painful than
usual, and she dreaded to go to bed and waken
Monsieur Jules with her moanings. The good man
was slumbering peacefully upstairs—she could hear
his lusty snores even where she sat—and it was a
shame to disturb him when he must rise so early.

So she sat in her little room at the end of the
counter, trying to knit by the light of a flickering
candle, and rocking back and forth in her chair
with a monotonous motion.

Suddenly the little bell tinkled and a gust of air
entered the shop, sending the mingled odors of
baked stuff whirling and scurrying about the room
in a most fragrant manner. Then the door closed,
and Madame laid down her knitting and turned to
greet the new-comer.

To her astonishment, it proved to be Ali Dubh.
His brown cheeks were flushed, and his glittering
black eyes roamed swiftly over the shop before they
turned full upon the Madame's calm face.

"Good!" he exclaimed, "you are alone."

"It is too late for trade. I am going to bed
presently," said Madame.

"I am in great trouble, and you must help me,"
returned the Arab, hastily. "Lock your door and

come with me into your little room, so that no one can see us through the street windows."

Madame hesitated. The request was unusual, and she knew nothing of the Arab's history. But she reflected that if the man attempted robbery or other mischief she could summon Monsieur Jules with a cry. Also, her interest had been aroused by Ali Dubh's queer behavior during the day.

While she thought the matter over the Arab himself locked the street door and hurried into the little room, where Madame composedly joined him a moment later.

"How can I help you?" she asked, picking up her knitting again.

"Listen!" said the Arab. "I must tell you all. You must know the truth!" He put his hand in a pocket of his loose robe and drew out a small flask. It was no bigger than two fingers and was made of pure gold, upon which strange characters had been richly engraved.

"This," said the Arab, in a low, impressive voice, "is the Great Elixir!"

"What does that mean?" asked Madame, glancing at the flask doubtfully.

"The Great Elixir? Ah, it is the Essence of

16

The Great Elixir

Vitality, the Water of Life — the Greatest Thing in all the World!"

"I don't understand," said Madame.

"Not understand? Why, a drop of the priceless liquid which this Golden Flask contains, if placed upon your tongue, would send new life coursing through your veins. It would give you power, strength, vitality greater than youth itself!

The Great Elixir

You could do anything — accomplish wonders — perform miracles — if you but tasted this precious liquid!"

"How odd!" exclaimed Madame, beginning to feel bewildered. And then she asked: "Where did you get it?"

"Ah! that is the story. That is what you must know," answered Ali Dubh. "It is centuries old, the Great Elixir. There is no more of it in all the world. The contents of this flask came into the keeping of the Ancestor of the Chief of my Tribe — whom we call a Shiek — and has been handed down from father to son as an heirloom more priceless than diamonds. The Chief of my Tribe, its last owner, carried the flask always hidden in his breast. But one day, when he and I were hunting together, a mad camel trampled the Shiek to his death, and with his last breath he gave the Great Elixir into my keeping. The Shiek had no son, and the flask was really mine. But many other Arab Shieks longed for the treasure and sought to gain it. So I escaped and wandered over the world. I came here, thinking I was safe from pursuit. But they have followed me!"

"All the way from Arabia?" asked Madame.

"Yes. To-day I saw them. They know my

lodgings. They are secretly hidden near, and before morning I know they plot to kill me and secure the Great Elixir. But for a time 1 have escaped them. I came here unseen. You must help me. You must take charge of the Great Elixir and keep it safely for me."

"Nonsense!" cried Madame, becoming aroused at last.

"Do not say that, I beg of you," exclaimed the eager Arab. "You are honest—I know you are! And they will never suspect you of having the Golden Flask."

"Perhaps not," said Madame, "and then, again, they may. My business is to tend the shop, and I am not going to get myself killed by a lot of desperate foreigners just to oblige *you*, Monsieur Ali Dubh! Take your Great Elixir to some one else. I don't want it."

For a minute the Arab seemed in despair. Then his face suddenly brightened.

"You suffer from rheumatism, do you not?" he asked.

"Yes, it's pretty bad to-night," she replied.

"Then I will cure it! I will cure your pains forever if you will keep my precious Elixir in secret until I come to reclaim it."

19

The Great Elixir

Madame hesitated, for just then she had a very bad twinge indeed.

"You think you can cure my pains?" she asked.

"I know it!" declared the Arab. He put his hand in a pocket and drew out another flask—a mate to the one containing the Great Elixir; only this was made of solid silver instead of gold.

"This flask," said Ali Dubh, "contains a positive cure for rheumatism. It will not fail. It never has failed. Take it and use it to make yourself well. Five drops in a bowl of water are enough. Bathe well the limbs that ache, and all pain will be gone forever. Accept it, gracious Madame, and keep for me the other flask in safe hiding until my enemies have gone away."

Madame was a practical woman, and it seemed an easy thing to do as the Arab desired. If she could get relief from those dreadful pains it would be well worth while to undertake a little trouble and responsibility by caring for Ali Dubh's other and more precious flask.

"Very well," said she. "I agree."

The Arab's face flushed with joy.

"Good," he cried; "I am saved! Guard well my precious flask—the one of gold. Show it to no one—not even to your good husband. Remember

20

that diamonds and rubies could not buy the Great
Elixir—the marvelous Essence of Vitality.   As for
the silver flask, I give it to you freely.   Its contents will cure all your ailments.   And now, good
night, and may Allah bless you!"

Swiftly he stole from the room, unlocked the
street door and vanished into the darkness.   And
Madame sat looking thoughtfully at the flasks.

The Two Flasks

Presently she remembered that the front door was yet unlocked. So she trotted out into the shop, bolted the door securely, drew down the curtains, and put out the dim light that had burned over the counter. Then Madame returned to the little room and looked at the two flasks again.

Aside from her rheumatism the good lady had one other physical weakness; she was color-blind. That is, she could seldom distinguish one color from another, and was quite liable to think blue was green and green was yellow. Many people have this trouble with their eyes; but it never had bothered Madame especially in waiting upon her customers.

Now, however, when she came back into her room and gazed at the two flasks upon her table, she had no idea which one was of gold and which of silver, for the weakness of her eyes prevented her from telling them apart by means of their color.

"Let me see," she murmured; "this must be

the flask which the Arab first drew from his pocket. No—I think *this* was the one." But the more she hesitated the more confused she became, and in the end she told herself honestly that she had not the faintest clue to guide her in knowing which flask contained the Essence of Vitality and which the cure for rheumatism.

And the pains were now so bad that she was anxious to cure them without a moment's delay.

The engraving on the two flasks was nearly the same; and if some of those queer foreign characters really differed, Madame did not know it. Also in size and shape the flasks were exactly alike. Truly Madame was in a fine quandary, and there seemed no way of getting out of it with safety.

She had almost decided to hide both flasks until the Arab returned, when several sharp twinges of pain caught her and made her long most earnestly for relief. If she went to bed now she would be sure to suffer all night, and in one of the flasks was a sure cure.

"I'll guess at it, and take the chances!" declared Madame, firmly. And then, choosing at haphazard, she hid the silver flask behind the mirror and put the gold one in her pocket. Afterward she picked up the lamp and walked as silently as possible through the short passage that led to Monsieur Jules' bake-room.

The big place was still and dark, and the little lamp only brightened a small part of it. But Madame did not care for that. Those pains were getting extremely hard to bear, and she had even ceased to care whether or not she had selected the right flask.

Taking a brown bowl from the shelf she drew it nearly full of water and then placed it upon a corner of the long, white mixing-table, beside the

lamp. Next she took the golden flask from her pocket.

"How much did the Arab say to put in the water?" she wondered, pausing in perplexed thought. "I declare, I've actually forgotten! But he said it was sure to cure me,

24

so I may as well use all the flask contains. For, after I am cured, I shall not need any more of it."

Reasoning thus, Madame removed the stopper and poured into the bowl every drop of that precious Elixir which Ali Dubh had prized more than life itself, and which his wild countrymen had come all the way from Arabia to America to possess. For generation after generation the priceless liquor had been preserved with jealous care, and now the baker's wife was rubbing it upon her limbs in an endeavor to cure the pangs of rheumatism!

She used very little of the contents of the bowl, after all. The touch of the Elixir upon her skin, although it was diluted with so much water, sent a glow of exhilaration throughout all her stout body.

The pains were suddenly eased, and Madame began to feel as light and airy as a fairy, in spite of her great mass of flesh.

It occurred to her that she would like to dance; to run and shout, to caper about as she used to do as a girl. But soon her shrewd common sense returned, and she told herself this was but the effect of the wonderful medicine, and that the wisest thing she could do was to go to bed and sleep soundly while she might.

Being still somewhat bewildered, the good woman picked up the lamp, and, leaving the bowl containing the Elixir standing upon the table, mounted the stairs with lighter steps than she had known in years.

Five minutes later she was in bed, snoring as loudly as Monsieur Jules himself.

The Gingerbread Man

The baker awoke at three o'clock, and soon afterward came downstairs yawning and rubbing his eyes in his accustomed manner. For it is a real hardship to arise in the middle of the night and go to work, and Monsieur Jules sometimes regretted he was such a skillful baker; for any other profession would have allowed him to sleep until daylight. But the bread and rolls and gingerbread must be fresh and warm by breakfast time, or the people would be sadly disappointed; and the only possible way to get them ready was to start the work at three o'clock.

First, he lighted the big swinging lamps, which made the room bright as day, and then he built the fires in the great furnaces. Presently these last were roaring in a very business-like manner, and as soon as he heard the roar Monsieur Jules began to whistle. It was his custom, and kept him from getting lonesome while he worked.

27

The Gingerbread Man

Next he kneaded the bread, formed it into loaves, and placed them in long rows upon the slabs—ready for the oven. The rolls were then

mixed and kneaded, and it took a longer time to get them ready than it had the bread, for they were small and quite daintily shaped. But at last the important task was completed, and while they were rising and the ovens heating, Monsieur mixed his gingerbread and cakes.

Somehow, the work progressed very swiftly this morning, and after a time the baker found he had a good hour to spare before the ovens would be ready.

Then a sudden idea struck him.

"Why, to-day is the Fourth of July," he thought, "and that is a National Holiday. I think I will make a fine gingerbread man, such as I used to make in Paris, and put it in the shop window to attract attention. These Americans like enterprise, and they have never seen a gingerbread man, for I have not made one since I came to this country."

With Monsieur Jules, to think was to act, and scarcely had he spoken these words when he began to gather his material together for a great batch of gingerbread dough. For he resolved that the man he was about to make should be big enough and fine enough to arouse the wonder of all beholders.

He began by filling a great bowl with flour, and then rubbed into the flour some butter and lard. "That will make it short," said Monsieur, "although it is to be a tall man." Then he added some

molasses. "He will be a sweet fellow," thought
the baker, smiling at his own pleasantries. Then
he shock in the ginger and several fragrant spices,
and began mixing the dough into one great mass.

"It is too stiff," reflected the baker, a few moments later. "My man must not be stiff, for that
would render him disagreeable." He laughed at
the whimsical thought, and glancing around, saw
the brown bowl that Madame had left sitting upon
a corner of the table. It was nearly full of the
precious liquid, and Monsieur Jules, with his mind
intent upon his work, never stopped to wonder
how it came there. Perhaps he thought he had
himself unconsciously filled the bowl with water.
Anyway, he dumped all of the Essence of Vitality
—the Great Elixir which could never be duplicated
in all the world—into the mass of dough he was
preparing for his gingerbread man!

Monsieur merely noticed that the dough had now
become the proper consistency, and mixed easily.

Whistling merrily, he presently spread the huge
batch of dough upon the big table and began rolling it and working it into the shape he desired.

Ah, but Monsieur Jules Grogrande was a true
artist, although a baker! Under his skillful hands
the gingerbread man slowly but surely took form;

THEN A SUDDEN IDEA STRUCK HIM.

The Gingerbread Man

and the form was fully as large as that of a well-grown fourteen-year-old boy. But it was by no means a boy that Monsieur was forming with such care; it was, rather, the figure of a typical French gentleman, such as may seldom be met with elsewhere than on the boulevards of Paris. It was interesting to watch the figure grow: interesting, of course, to Monsieur Jules, as there was no one else in the bake-room to see.

The Gingerbread Man

The man appeared to be dressed in excellent fashion. Monsieur made him a collar and shirt-front of white bread dough, which looked very beautiful in contrast to the brown gingerbread-dough of his clothes. Then with a lump of dough, carefully kneaded, he formed the man's necktie, making a very artistic bow indeed. A waistcoat of fashionable cut was next added. The buttons on the man's coat were white lozenges, and to represent shoes the baker mixed his dough with licorice, until the shoes seemed as black and shiny as if freshly polished.

You would have loved to see, could you have been present, the delicate skill with which the clever baker carved the hands and fingers of his man, using a small but sharp knife, and patting and rounding each dough finger into proper shape. He even clipped from a sheet of transparent celluloid the finger-nails, and pressed them carefully into the dough at the ends of the fingers. Who but Monsieur would ever have thought of such a thing?

But, after all, it was upon the face that the baker exercised his best skill. As a sculptor forms his models out of clay, so Monsieur pressed and squeezed and molded his pliant dough, until every feature of the gingerbread man became wonder-

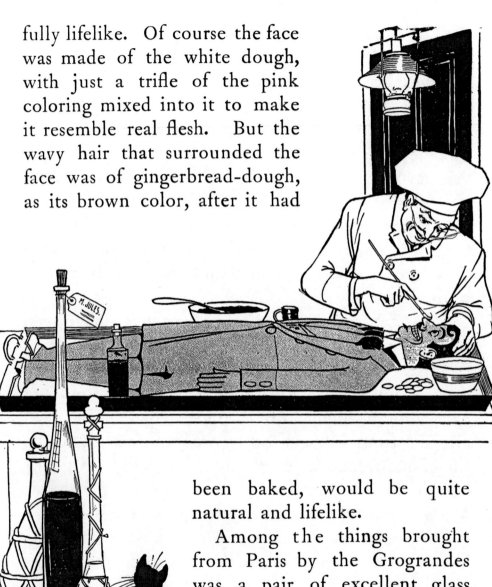

fully lifelike. Of course the face was made of the white dough, with just a trifle of the pink coloring mixed into it to make it resemble real flesh. But the wavy hair that surrounded the face was of gingerbread-dough, as its brown color, after it had

been baked, would be quite natural and lifelike.

Among the things brought from Paris by the Grograndes was a pair of excellent glass eyes, and Monsieur Jules rummaged in a drawer until he

34

found them, and then pressed them into the dough face. And now it positively seemed that the gingerbread man was looking at you, and the eyes lent its face a gentle and kindly expression.

"There's something lacking, however," murmured the baker, looking at his work critically. "Ah, I know—it's the teeth!"

Teeth for a gingerbread man! But nothing was easier to represent, once their absence was noted. Between the lips of the man our baker pressed two rows of small white candies, and it was wonderful to remark the pleasant smile that now lent its charm to the face.

With a sigh of satisfaction in the result of his work, the baker at last declared his gingerbread man ready for the oven.

"And it is my masterpiece!" cried Monsieur Jules, proudly. "Never, even in Paris, have I seen so perfect a man of dough. He is well worthy to have a name, and I will call him John Dough, which will be appropriate, indeed!"

But the great ovens were now glowing brightly, so Monsieur filled them with bread and rolls, and watched them carefully until the big and little loaves were all done to a turn. The cakes and cookies came next, and by the time that dawn arrived the front shop was stocked with heaps of the warm, fresh-smelling loaves and rolls, and trays of delicious cakes and buns, hot from the ovens.

Then the baker came back to his gingerbread man, which he first placed gently upon a great iron slab, and then slid it all into the open door of a perfectly heated oven.

With great anxiety Monsieur watched the oven. The dough was properly mixed, the workmanship was most excellent. Would the baking turn out to be as perfect as the rest? Much good dough may be spoiled in the baking. None knew that better than Jules Grogrande.

So he tended the oven with nervous care, and finally, at exactly the right moment, the baker threw open the oven door and drew out the sheet of iron upon which the great and grand gingerbread man rested.

He was baked to perfection!

Filled with pride and satisfaction, Monsieur bent admiringly over his great creation; and as he did so, the gingerbread man moved, bent his back, sat up, and looked about him with his glass eyes, while a wondering expression crept over his face.

"Dear me!" said he, "isn't it very warm and close in this room?"

The Gingerbread Man

The Great Elixir had accomplished its purpose. The wonderful Essence of Vitality, prized for centuries and closely guarded, had lent its marvelous powers of energy, strength, and life to a gingerbread man! And all through the stupidity of a baker's wife who was color-blind and could not distinguish a golden flask from a silver one!

Monsieur Jules, who knew nothing of the Arab's flasks, or of the Great Elixir, glared wildly into the glass eyes of the gingerbread man. He was at first sure that his own eyes, and also his ears, had played him a trick.

"John Dough—John Dough!" he cried, "did you speak? Merciful heavens! Did you speak, John Dough?"

"I did," said the gingerbread man, struggling to rise from the slab, "and I declare that it *is* warm and close in this room!"

Monsieur Jules gave a scream of terror. Then he turned and fled.

A moment later he staggered into the shop, tossed his hands above his head, and fell in a heap upon the floor—being overcome by a fainting spell.

Madame, who had just come downstairs and opened the shop, gazed upon her husband's terrified actions with an amazement that prevented her from moving a limb or uttering a sound.

What in the world could have happened to Jules?

Then she received the greatest shock of her life.

From out the door of the bake-room came a gingerbread man, so fresh from the oven that the odor of hot gingerbread surrounded him like a cloud. He looked neither to right nor left, but picked Monsieur's tall silk hat from off a peg and placed it carelessly upon his own head. Next he caught up a large candy cane from a show-case,

MONSIEUR JULES TURNED AND FLED.

stepped over the prostrate body of the baker, and
so left the shop, closing the front door behind him.

Madame saw him passing the windows, stepping
along briskly and
swinging the cane in
his left hand.

Then the good lady
imitated her husband's
example. She gave a

shrill scream, threw up
her hands, and tumbled
over unconscious.

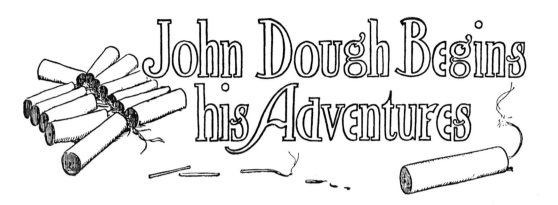

John Dough Begins his Adventures

Now, when John Dough left Madame Grogrande's shop and wandered up the street, he was reeking with the delightful odor of fresh gingerbread. Indeed, he was still so hot from the oven that I am positive you could not have held your hand against him for more than a second. The Great Elixir had brought him to life, and given him a certain standing in the world; but during the first half-hour of his existence John Dough was very hot-headed. Also he was hot-footed, for he discovered that, by walking fast, the contact with the fresh morning air drew the heat from his body and made him feel much more comfortable.

One virtue lent by the Great Elixir was knowledge, and while John Dough felt that he possessed unlimited knowledge (having had an overdose of the Elixir), he could not very well apply it to his surroundings because he lacked experience with the world, which alone renders knowledge of any value to mankind. John Dough could speak all languages—modern and classic. He had a logical and clear mind—what is called a "level head," you know; and this was coupled with good sense, fair judgment, and a tangled mass of wisdom that had been dumped into him in a haphazard fashion.

But these rare qualities were as yet of no use to our man because he had acquired no experience. It was like putting tools into a scholar's hands and asking him to make a watch. John Dough might accomplish wonders in time, if he did not grow stale and crumble; but just now he was the freshest individual that ever came out of a bake-room.

It was still early morning, and most folks were in bed. A prowling dog smelled the gingerbread and came trotting up with the intention of having a bite of it; but John Dough raised his candy cane and hit the dog a clip on the end of its nose that sent the animal in another direction with its tail between its legs. Then, whistling merrily, the gingerbread man walked on. He knew no tune whatever, but he could whistle, and so he managed to express an erratic mixture of notes that would have made Herr Wagner very proud.

His flesh (or bread, rather) was cooling off beautifully now. He was growing hard and crisp and felt much more substantial than at first. The baker had made him light and the Elixir had made him strong and vigorous. A great future lay before John Dough, if no accident happened to him.

Presently some one said, "Hello!" John stopped short, for in front of him stood a bright-eyed boy with a piece of lighted punk in one hand and a bunch of firecrackers in the other. It was Ned Robbins, who had been up since daybreak celebrating the Glorious Fourth.

"You skeered me at first," said the boy, with a look of amazement that he tried to cover with a laugh.

"I beg your pardon, I'm sure," returned John Dough, politely.

43

"Been to a masquerade?" asked Ned, staring hard at the gingerbread man.

"No, indeed," replied the other. "I am not disguised, I assure you. You see me as I am."

"G'wan!" exclaimed Ned. But he could smell the gingerbread, and he began to grow frightened. So he touched the punk to the fuse of his biggest firecracker, dropped it on the ground at the feet of John Dough, and then turned and scampered up an alley as fast as he could go.

The gingerbread man stood still and looked after Ned until the cracker suddenly exploded with a bang that caused John's candy teeth to chatter. His whole body was terribly jarred and he nearly fell backward in the shock of surprise. Then he, also, started to run. It was not fear, so much as ignorance of what might happen next, that caused him to fly from the spot; but he ran with a speed that was simply wonderful, considering that his limbs were of gingerbread. Truly, that Arabian Elixir was a marvelous thing!

Bang! He had run plump into another group of boys, knocking two of them over before they could get out of his way. His silk hat was jammed over his eyes and the candy cane struck the wheel of a toy cannon and broke off a good two inches from its end.

44

THE CRACKER SUDDENLY EXPLODED

John Dough Begins His Adventures

As he pulled off his hat he heard a shout and saw the boys all scrambling for the broken end of the candy cane. One of them grabbed it and ran away, and the others followed in a mad chase and were soon out of sight.

John Dough looked after them wonderingly.

John Dough Begins His Adventures

Then he drew himself up, pulled down his fine vest, sighed at discovering a slight crack in his shirt-front, and walked slowly along the street again. His first experience of life was not altogether pleasant.

"Good gracious!" said a voice.

He paused, and saw a woman leaning over a gate beside him and glaring at him in mingled surprise and terror. She held a broom in her hand, for she had been sweeping the walk. John lifted his hat politely.

"Good morning, madam," said he.

"Why, it's really alive!" gasped the woman.

"Is a live person so very unusual?" asked John, curiously.

"Surely, when he's made of cake!" answered the woman, still staring as if she could not believe her eyes.

"Pardon me; I am not cake, but gingerbread," he answered, in a rather dignified way.

"It's all the same," she answered. "You haven't any right to be alive. There's no excuse for it."

"But how can I help it?" he asked, somewhat puzzled by this remark.

"Oh, I don't suppose it's your fault. But it isn't right, you know. Who made you?"

John Dough Begins His Adventures

"Jules Grogrande, the baker," he said, for he had read the name over the door.

"I always knew there was something wrong with those Frenchies," she declared. "Are you done?"

Before he could reply she had drawn a large straw from the broom and stuck it several inches into his side.

"Don't do that!" he cried, indignantly, as she drew out the bit of broom again.

"I was only tryin' you," she remarked. "You're done to a turn, and ought to make good eating while you're fresh."

John gazed at her in horror.

"Good eating!" he cried; "woman, would you murder me?"

"I can't say it would be exactly murder," she replied, looking at him hungrily.

"To destroy life is murder!" he said, sternly.

"But to destroy gingerbread isn't," she rejoined. "And I can't see that it's cannibalism to eat a man if he happens to be cake, and fresh baked. And that frosting looks good. Come inside while I get a knife."

She opened the gate and tried to grab John Dough by an arm. But he gave a sudden backward leap and then sped down the street at a furi-

48

"COME INSIDE WHILE I GET A KNIFE"

ous run, looking neither to right nor left in his eager flight.

Luckily, he was not in the center of the town, but near the outskirts, and the houses were few and scattered.

By and by he saw a deserted barn near the roadside. The door was half open and sagged on its hinges, so it could not be closed.

John darted into the barn and hid behind some hay in the far side. He was thoroughly frightened, and believed he must avoid mingling with the people of the town if he would escape instant destruction.

A knife! A knife! The word kept ringing in his ears and filled him with horror. A knife could slice him into pieces easily. He imagined himself sliced and lying on a plate ready for hungry folks to eat, and the picture made him groan aloud.

All through the day he kept securely hidden behind the hay. Toward evening he decided to revisit the bakery. It was a difficult task, for he had passed through many streets and lanes without noticing where he was going, and it grew darker every minute. But at last, just as he was beginning to despair, he saw a dim light in a window and read over the door the sign: "Jules Grogrande, Baker."

John Dough Begins His Adventures

He opened the door so softly that the little bell scarcely tinkled. But no one would have heard it had it rung loudly, for there was a confused murmer of fierce voices coming from the little room Madame usually occupied.

John Dough skipped behind the counter, where he could see into the room without being seen himself.

Around the little table stood the Arab, Monsieur Jules, and Madame, and they were all staring angrily into each other's faces.

"But the flask!" cried Ali Dubh. "Where is my precious flask?"

"It is here," said Madame, reaching behing the mirror and drawing forth something that glittered in the lamp-light.

"But this is the silver flask—the cure for rheumatism," exclaimed the Arab. "Where is my Golden Flask—containing the priceless Elixir of Life?"

John Dough Begins His Adventures

"I must have made a mistake," said Madame, honestly; "for my eyes are so queer that I cannot tell gold from silver. Anyway, the contents of the other flask I emptied into a bowl of water, and rubbed my limbs with it."

The Arab shouted a despairing cry in his native tougue and then glared wildly at the woman.

"Was it the brown bowl, Leontine?" asked Monsieur Jules, trembling with excitement.

"Yes," she answered.

"Where is it? Where is it?" demanded the Arab, in a hoarse voice. "The precious liquor may yet be saved."

"Too late, Monsieur," said the baker, shaking his head, sadly. "I used the contents of the bowl to mix the dough for my gingerbread man."

"A gingerbread man! What do you mean?" asked Ali Dubh.

"I baked a man out of gingerbread this morning,"  said Monsieur Jules, "and to my horror he came alive, and spoke to me, and walked out of the shop while he was still smoking hot."

"It is no wonder," said

the Arab, dolefully; for within him was enough of the Great Elixir to bring a dozen men to life, and give them strength and energy for many years. Ah, Monsieur and Madame, think of what your stupidity has cost the world!"

"I do not comprehend," said Madame, firmly, "how the world has ever yet been benefited by the Great Elixir, which you and your selfish country-men have kept for centuries corked up in a golden flask."

"Bismillah!" shouted the Arab, striking himself fiercely across the forehead with his clinched fist. "Cannot you understand, you stupid one, that it was mine—*mine!*—this Wonderful Water of Life? I had planned to use it myself—drop by drop—that I might live forever."

"I'm sorry," said Monsieur; "but it is your own fault. You forced my wife to care for the flask, and you would not let her tell me about it. So, through your own stupidity, I used it in the gingerbread man."

"Ah!" said Ali Dubh, an eager gleam in his eyes, "where, then, is that same gingerbread man? If I can find him, and eat him, a bit at a time, I shall get the benefit of the Great Elixir after all! It would not be so powerful, perhaps, as in its natural state; but it would enable me to live for many, many years!"

John Dough heard this speech with a thrill of horror. Also he now began to understand how he happened to be alive.

"I do not know where the gingerbread man is," said Monsieur. "He walked out of my shop while he was quite hot."

"But he can be found," said the Arab. "It is impossible for a gingerbread man, who is alive, to escape notice. Come, let us search for him at once! I must find him and eat him."

He fairly dragged Monsieur and Madame from the room in his desperation, and John Dough crouched out of sight behind the counter until he

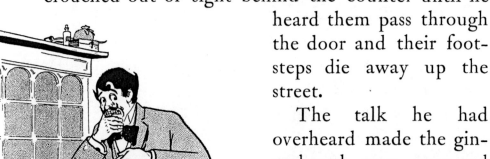

heard them pass through the door and their footsteps die away up the street.

The talk he had overheard made the gingerbread man very sad indeed. The bakery was no safe home for him, after all. Evidently it was the Arab's intention

John Dough Begins His Adventures

to find him and insist upon eating him; and John Dough did not want to be eaten at all.

Therefore his enemies must not find him. They were no safer to meet with than the awful woman who wanted to cut him into slices; and he was learning, by degrees, that all men were dangerous enemies to him, although he had himself the form of a man.

He left the bakery and stole out into the street once more, walking now in the opposite direction from that taken by the Arab and the Grograndes.

As he hurried along he met with few people on the streets; and these, in the dark, paid little attention to the gingerbread man; so gradually his spirits rose and his confidence in his future returned.

By and by he heard a strange popping and hissing coming from the direction of the square in the center of the town, and then he saw red and green lights illuminating the houses, and fiery comets go sailing into the sky to break into dozens of beautiful colored stars.

The people were having their Fourth of July fireworks, and John Dough became curious to witness the display from near by. So, forgetting his fears, he ran through the streets until he came to a big crowd of people, who were too busy watching the fireworks to notice that a gingerbread man stood beside them.

John Dough pressed forward until he was quite in the front row, and just behind the men who were firing the rockets.

For a time he watched the rush of the colored fires with much pleasure, and thoroughly enjoyed the sputtering of a big wheel that refused to go around, merely sending out weak and listless spurts of green and red sparks, as is the manner of such wheels.

But now the event of the evening was to occur. Two men brought out an enormous rocket, fully fifteen feet tall and filled with a tremendous charge of powder. This they leaned against a wooden trough that stood upright; but the rocket was too tall to stay in place, and swayed from side to side awkwardly.

"Here! Hold that stick!" cried one of the men, and John Dough stepped forward and grasped the stick of the big rocket firmly, not knowing there was any danger in doing so.

Then the man ran to get a piece of rope to tie the rocket in place; but the other man, being excited and thinking the rocket was ready to fire,

JOHN DOUGH IS CARRIED OFF BY THE ROCKET 57

John Dough Begins His Adventures

touched off the fuse without noticing that John Dough was clinging fast to the stick.

There was a sudden shriek, a rush of fire, and then — slowly at first, but with ever-increasing speed — the huge rocket mounted far into the sky, carrying with it the form of the gingerbread man!

Chick, the Cherub

The rocket continued to send out fiery sparks of burning powder as it plunged higher and higher into the black vault of the heavens; but few of these came in contact with John Dough, who clung to the far side of the stick and so escaped being seriously damaged. Also the rocket curved, and presently sped miles away over land and sea, impelled by the terrible force of the powder it contained. John fully expected that it would burst presently, and blow him to bits amid a cloud of colored stars. But the giant rocket was not made in the same way as the other and smaller ones that had been fired, the intention being merely to make it go as high and as far as possible. So it finally burned itself out; but so great was the speed it had attained that it continued to fly for many minutes after the last spark had died away.

Then the rocket began to take a downward course; but it was so high up, by that time, that the stick and the empty shell flew onward hour

59

after hour, gradually nearing the ground, until finally, just as a new day began to break, the huge stick, with John Dough still holding fast to its end, fell lightly upon an island washed on all sides by the waves of a mighty sea.

John fell on a soft bush, and thence bounded to the ground, where for a time he lay quite still and tried to recover his thoughts.

He had not done much thinking, it seems, while he was in the air. The rush of wind past his ears had dazed him, and he only realized he must cling fast to the stick and await what might happen. Indeed, that was the only thing to be done in such an emergency.

The shock of the fall had for a moment dazed the ginger-bread man; and as he lay upon the ground he heard a voice cry:

"Get off from me! Will you? Get off, I say."

John rolled over and sat up, and then another person—a little man with a large head—also sat up and faced him.

"What do you mean by it?" asked the little man, glaring upon John Dough angrily. "Can't you see where you're falling?"

"No," answered John.

It was growing lighter every minute, and the gray mists of morning were fading away before the rising sun. John looked around him and saw he was upon a broad, sandy beach which the waves of a great sea lapped peacefully. Behind was a green meadow, and then mountains that rose high into the air.

"How did you happen to be where I fell?" he asked, turning to the little man again.

"I always sleep on the sands," replied the other, wagging his head solemnly. "It's my fad. Fresh air, you know. I'm called the 'Fresh-Air Fiend.' I suppose you're a new inhabitant. You seem rather queer."

"I'm made of gingerbread," said John.

"Well, that certainly is unusual, so I've no doubt you will be warmly welcomed in our Island," replied the man.

"But where am I?" asked John, looking around again with a puzzled expression.

"This is the Isle of Phreex," answered the other, "and it is inhabited by unusual people. I'm one, and you're another."

He made such a droll face as he said this that the gingerbread man could not resist smiling, but it startled him to hear another laugh at his back — a sound merry and sweet, such as a bird trills. He swung around quickly and saw a child standing upon the sands, where the rays of the sun fell brightly upon its little form. And then the glass eyes of the gingerbread man grew big, and stood out from his cake face in a way that fully expressed his astonishment.

"It's a Vision!" he exclaimed.

"No, it's the Cherub — whom we call Chick," answered the big-headed man, carelessly.

The child had fair hair, falling in fleecy waves to its shoulders, but more or less tangled and neglected. It had delicate features, rosy cheeks, and round blue eyes. When these eyes were grave — which was seldom — there were questions in them; when they smiled — which was often — sunbeams rippled over their blue surfaces. For clothing the child wore garments of pure white, which reached from the neck to the ankles, and had wide flowing sleeves and legs, like those of a youngster's pajamas. The

"IT'S THE CHERUB"

63

little one's head and feet were bare, but the pink soles were protected by sandals fastened with straps across the toes and ankles.

"Good morning," said John, again smiling and hoping he had not stared too rudely. "It gives me great pleasure to meet you."

"My name's Chick," replied the child, laughing in sweet trills, while the blue eyes regarded the gingerbread man with evident wonder.

"That's a funny name," said John.

"Yes, it *is* funny," the child agreed, with a friendly nod. "Chick means a chicken, you know. But I'm not a chicken."

"Of course not," returned John. "A chicken is covered with feathers. And you are not."

At this Chick laughed merrily, and said, as if it were the simplest thing in the world: "I'm the Incubator Baby, you know."

"Dear me, I hadn't the least idea of it," John answered gravely. "May I ask what an Incubator Baby is?"

64

The child squatted down in the sand, hugged its chubby knees, and uttered peal after peal of joyous laughter.

"How funny!" it gurgled; "how funny that you don't know what the Incubator Baby is! Really, you must be fresh-baked!"

"I am," said John, feeling rather ashamed to acknowledge the fact, but resolving to be truthful.

"Then, of course, you are very ignorant," remarked the Fresh-Air Fiend, rubbing his big head complacently.

"Oh, as for that," said John, "I acquired, in course of manufacture, a vast deal of ancient learning, which I got from an Arabian Elixir with which the baker mixed me. I am well posted in all events down to the last century, but I cannot recall any knowledge of an Incubator Baby."

"No, they're a recent invention," declared the big-headed man, patting tenderly the child's golden curls. "Were you, by any chance, at the Pan-American Exposition? Or the Lousiana Purchase Exposition?"

"No," answered John. "My knowledge was corked up about then."

"Well," continued the man, "there were a good many Incubator Babies at both those expositions, and lots of people saw them. But Chick is the first and only Original Incubator Baby, and so Chick properly belongs in the Isle of Phreex."

Chick jumped up, made a stiff bow, and with eyes sparkling with mischief exclaimed: "I'm six years old and quite strong and well."

"Tut-tut, Chick!" remonstrated the big-headed man; "it was more than two years ago you were taught to make that speech. You can't be always six years old, you know."

The little sprite enjoyed the joke so much that John was forced to laugh in sympathy. But just then a thought struck him, and he asked, a little nervously:

"Do you like gingerbread?"

"I don't know," replied Chick. "Are you gingerbread?"

"I am," said John, bravely.

"Then I like gingerbread," the child declared; "for you smell sweet and look kind and gentle."

John didn't know whether to accept this as a compliment or not. He was sorry to learn that he smelled sweet, although to be called kind and gentle was grateful praise.

"Some folks," he remarked, timidly, "have an idea they like to *eat* gingerbread."

66

"I couldn't eat you," the child said, seriously, "because, being the Incubator Baby, I have to be very careful of my diet. You might not agree with me."

"I'm sure I couldn't agree with any one who ate me," John declared. "For, although as yet I have had no experience of that sort, it seems to me a very undesirable fate."

"Very true," remarked the big-headed man.

"Let's be friends!" exclaimed Chick, coming close to John and taking his soft brown hand in a firm clasp. "I'll take care of you."

John looked down at the merry little elf in positive wonder.

"We'll be friends, all right," said he; "but instead of your taking care of me, Chick, I'll take care of you."

"Oh, there you are entirely wrong," broke in the big-headed man. "Chick's a privileged character in the Isle of Phreex, and the only one of us who dares defy our awful kinglet. And in case of danger——"

"Danger!" cried John, with a start. "Is there danger here, too?"

Chick's laughter rang out at the foolish question, but the man replied seriously:

"There is danger everywhere, to those who are unusual, and especially in the Isle of Phreex, where we are at the mercy of a horrid kinglet. But come; we must go and report your arrival to that same graceless ruler, or we shall all be punished."

"Very well," said John, meekly.

But as he took Chick's hand and turned to depart the Fresh-Air Fiend uttered an exclamation of annoyance, and said:

"Here's bad luck already! The Failings are coming this way."

As he spoke a noise of shouting and chattering reached their ears, and presently several people came around a corner of rock and stood before John and his newly found friends.

"It's the Brotherhood of Failings," whispered the big-headed man. "Look out for them, or they'll do you a mischief."

"Don't worry; I'll take care of you," said Chick, pressing the dough hand.

John stared at the new-comers, and they returned the compliment by staring at him. A queerer lot of folks could seldom have been seen together.

"This is the Blunderer," said the Fresh-Air Fiend, indicating a short, fat man who was clothed in glittering armor and bore a lance over his shoulder.

THE BROTHERHOOD OF FAILINGS

The Blunderer acknowledged the introduction by bowing. "And here is the Thoughtless One," continued the man, pointing to a tall, lean man who was clothed in chamois-leather and carried a wide-mouthed blunderbuss under his arm.

"Look out for the gun," said Chick; "he never knows whether or not it is loaded."

"And here are the Disagreeable, and the Unlucky, and the Sorrowful, and the Ugly, and the Awkward," continued the big-headed man, pointing out each Failing in turn. "Their peculiarities you will have no trouble to discover. Indeed, on all the Isle of Phreex, there is no one more unpleasant to meet with than this same lot of Failings."

At this the Brothers all bowed, saying at the same time:

"We are proud of ourselves!"

At that instant the Awkward tripped over his own toes and fell against the Blunderer, who tumbled headlong and thrust his slim lance straight through the body of John Dough.

"Oh!" cried Chick, greatly horrified.

"I told you so!" growled the Fresh-Air Fiend, pulling out the lance hastily. "Tell me, John Dough, are you dead, or are you just dying?"

"Neither one," said John, ruefully pushing

together the hole that the lance had made; "but it doesn't add to my personal appearance to be prodded in that fashion. I'm made of gingerbread," he explained, turning to the man in armor.

"I beg your pardon! I really beg your pardon! ' said the Blunderer, greatly distressed at what he had done. "I had no intention of hurting you."

"He means well," said the Incubator Baby; but that doesn't help much."

"He won't last long in this Island," grunted the Bad-Tempered, referring to John Dough.

"Being made of gingerbread, he can't be expected to last," remarked the Disagreeable, smiling in a way that made John shudder.

"He shall have my protection," said the Blunderer. "It's the least I can do to make amends. Here—put on this armor!"

He hastily began stripping off the plates of metal, and placed the steel helmet over the head of the gingerbread man.

"No, no!" exclaimed John. "I don't want to wear all that hardware."

"But you must!" cried the Blunderer. "It's the only way you can escape accident in this awful Island."

"That's true enough," agreed the big-headed

man. "I advise you to wear the armor, my gingerbread friend."

So John submitted to being dressed in the armor, and no sooner had the plates been strapped upon him than the wisdom of the act was apparent. For there came a rush and whirl of sound, and sud-

denly a great monster swept over the sands at the very spot where they stood. It sent the Brotherhood of Failings sprawling in every direction, while the Incubator Baby flew to the water's edge, and John Dough's armor-clad body was knocked down and pressed into the soft sand until it was level with the surface.

But presently Chick came back and made the others dig him out and set him upon his feet again, and then it was seen that no one had been seriously injured.

"What was it?" asked John, gazing in amazement at the place where the monster had disappeared in the distance.

"It's the one-wheeled automobile," answered the Sorrowful, "and unless it gets smashed mighty soon the Isle of Phreex will be an Isle of Cripples. I don't understand why they license the thing."

"Why, to make room for new arrivals, of course," declared the Disagreeable. "But it was lucky for the Pudding Man that he happened to be dressed in steel."

"I am not pudding, if you please," said John, indignantly. "I beg you to remember that I am gingerbread."

"It's all one," remarked the Thoughtless, "your cake is dough, anyhow."

"Let us return to the castle," the Ugly said. "Our Kinglet should be introduced to his new subject."

So they all started off across the green, Chick leading the gingerbread man, until they came to a path leading upward through the rocks, along which they began to ascend. John had much difficulty in keeping out of the way of the Awkward, who tripped and stumbled constantly, while the Blunderer insisted upon taking the wrong path, and the Bad-Tempered stopped twice to fight with the Disagreeable and the Thoughtless. At last, however, they reached the top, which proved to be a broad plain of rock, upon which stood a great castle with many tall spires and grim towers and glittering minarets.

While they paused for John Dough to admire the view, and that they all might get breath, a sharp voice said near them:

"You're late, you lot of Failings, and the Kinglet will scold."

John looked around, and saw perched upon a point of rock beside the path a most curious looking creature.

"Don't stare!" it said, with a laugh. "*I* don't, and I've got a dozen eyes to your one. Let me introduce myself. I'm the Prize Potato from the Centerville Fair."

Indeed, John now noticed a big blue ribbon twined around the middle of the potato, and on the ribbon was printed in gold letters: "First Prize."

"Some day you'll sprout," said the Disagreeable, "and then you won't have so many eyes."

The Prize Potato winked its numerous eyes, one after the other, in a droll fashion, and answered:

74

THE CASTLE OF PHREEX

"Some day you'll meet with an accident, my dear Failing; but when you're planted in the ground you'll not sprout at all. That's where I'm your superior, for I'm perpetual. Every one of my eyes is good for a half-peck of potatoes, at least."

"Unless you're boiled with your jacket on," remarked the Ugly, with a sour smile.

"Come, come! Let us on," interrupted the little man with the big head. "Our Kinglet doubtless awaits us."

When they had gone a few steps farther the Incubator Baby paused to say: "Some one is following us, and it's a stranger."

This remark caused John to look around, and immediately he stopped short with an expression of horror upon his frosted face. For there, turning the corner of the rocky path, was Ali Dubh the Arab. The fellow at once uttered a yell of joy and triumph, and drawing his gleaming knife he rushed upon John Dough with great eagerness.

The gingerbread man had given up all hope of escape and stood tremblingly awaiting his foe when, Chick suddenly grasped the Blunderer's lance and tripped the Arab so neatly with it that Ali Dubh fell his full length upon the path and broke his

knife-blade into a dozen pieces. But he squirmed
forward and was about to bite into John's leg when
the big-headed man came to the rescue and threw
a handful of pebbles into the Arab's open mouth,
and so prevented him from doing the gingerbread
man any damage.

"He seems dangerous," remarked the Blunderer.
"Let's tie him up, before he hurts some one."

So while the Arab was coughing the pebbles out
of his mouth, the Brotherhood of Failings bound

77

his hands and feet with strong cords, so that he could not move.

"He's mine!" shouted the Arab, as soon as he could speak. "He belongs to me. I claim him for my own."

"There's no harm in that," replied the Fresh-Air Fiend. "But one of the laws of this Isle is that no person shall be injured by any one except the king-let. And every one here must obey the laws. So, unless you promise not to carve or to eat this man of gingerbread, who is now a subject of our king-let, we must lock you up in prison."

"I'll eat him as soon as I have the chance. I have a right to do so," cried the Arab.

"You're a bad man!" said Chick, stamping one small foot indignantly.

"I'm not," answered Ali Dubh; "I'm a good man. And I paid Jules Grogrande fifty cents for this gingerbread imitation of a man, who is mixed with my own magic Elixir. Also I paid a witch nine dollars to transport me to wherever the gin-gerbread man might be — which is right here — that I might take possession of my own property. So I've got him, and he's paid for, and he's mine, and I claim the right to eat him whenever I please."

"You'll do no such thing," declared Chick.

"Why, John Dough is alive, and no one has a right to make him dead and then eat him — even if he *is* paid for!"

"Don't worry, my Cherub," said the big-headed man, soothingly; "we'll go at once and lock this

Arab in a strong room of the castle, so that he can't possibly escape."

Chick smiled sweetly at this promise; but the Arab scowled and said, grimly:

"Never mind. My time will come. Some day

I shall surely eat that gingerbread man, in spite of this Cherub and all the rest of you."

This defiance made the Brotherhood of Failings and the big-headed man so angry that they at once dragged Ali Dubh away to the castle, and John Dough and Chick followed after, hand in hand, and feeling quite safe.

Presently they came to a great archway that led into the courtyard of the castle. Having passed through this arch, the gingerbread man saw groups of the most astonishing people, who were busying themselves over extraordinary tasks, such as building machines, boiling strange-smelling chemicals in queer pots, drawing curious designs, and like occupations. A sudden crash announced that the Blunderer had fallen into the middle of a delicate machine and smashed it into bits. Before they could pull him out the Unlucky One ran against the whirling arm of a windmill and was tossed halfway across the courtyard, while the Awkward One upset a boiling kettle and set every one to coughing who inhaled the odor of the compound that was spilled upon the ground.

To John's surprise no one seemed much worried over these accidents. Even the victims joined in Chick's merry laughter, and those of the Failings who had escaped disaster calmly proceeded to lock up the Arab in a cell that had a strong iron grating for a door, and fastened with a huge padlock.

Afterward they all entered through a second arch into the great hall of the castle.

This was a long, wide room with a tiled floor, and walls that were covered with many trophies, such as armor, spears, battle-axes, and swords of ancient design.

At the farther end was a raised platform upon which stood a gorgeous throne. Back of the throne was an electric sign, flashing one letter at a time, and reading: "What is Home without a Kinglet?" Over the throne was suspended an enormous crown —big enough for a giant—which sparkled with gems. Beside the throne a very fat man sat in a chair so low that his knees nearly touched his chin. He wore a short red coat, a wide white vest, and blue knee-breeches, and all were embroidered in gold. The fat man's eyes were closed and he seemed asleep.

Within the throne sat the kinglet, propped upon purple cushions, so that he would fit it better. For the kinglet was a small boy with a long, freckled face, blue eyes, a pug nose, and black hair banged across his forehead, and hanging in lank, straight

locks far down over his shoulders. He wore an
ermine cloak lined with purple, and bore in his
hand a sceptre with a jewelled ball at one end,
while beyond the ball projected a small golden
knob. The kinglet's slim legs were crossed under
him like those of a Turk, and he seemed very frail
and delicate.

However, when the Failings and the Fresh-Air
Fiend and Chick and John Dough entered, the
kinglet's brow was puckered into a frown, and his
blue eyes fairly flashed fire.

"Odds Zooks!" he cried, as they all knelt before
the throne, "why have you dared to wait until
this hour to pay me your devoirs?"

Then he leaned down and prodded the fat
man with the knob of his sceptre, so that the
sleeper started and opened his eyes. "Is that
right, Nebbie? Is 'devoir' a kingly word?" he
demanded.

"Absolutely kingly, your Majesty," said the fat
man, yawning. "It was used by King Arthur and
Richard Cœur de Leon."

"Very well!" said the kinglet, proudly. Then
he turned again to the kneeling group before him.
"Why don't you answer me?" he exclaimed. "Why
are you so late in paying me your boudoirs?"

THE KINGLET AND NEBBIE

"Devoirs, your Majesty!" said the fat man, hastily.

"I said 'devoirs'!" returned the kinglet, turning upon him in anger.

"We are late because we did not get here sooner," said the Awkward; "and we could not get here sooner because we were late."

"So!" shrieked his Majesty, with blazing eyes. "Now by my halidom——" he paused suddenly, and turned to the fat man, prodding him so fiercely that he jumped several feet into the air. "Is 'halidom' the right word, Nebbie?"

"Sure," said the fat man, nodding emphatically.

"What does it mean?" asked the kinglet.

"What does halidom mean?"

"Yes."

"Why, a halidom is a halidom," said the fat man, thoughtfully; "and belongs to kings."

"But what *is* it?" persisted the kinglet, impatiently.

"It's a——a——a sort of a royal prerogative, and is usually painted red," returned the fat man, and immediately resumed his seat and closed his eyes again.

The kinglet sighed, and turned anew to the Failings.

"Let me see," he remarked; "where was I?"

"You were by your halidom, your Majesty," suggested the Blunderer.

"Oh, yes." Again the long freckled face took on a frown. "By my halidom, churl—" He stopped to glance at the fat man.

"Churl is all right," mumbled Nebbie, without opening his eyes.

"By my halidom, churl, you shall either swallow my sceptre or die the death!"

"What death?" asked the Blunderer, trembling.

"The one that makes people dead," replied the kinglet, sternly. "Choose, then, varlet—" ("Varlet is good," said Nebbie, quickly, to avoid a thrust) "whether to swallow my sceptre or die the death!"

The Blunderer glanced at the sceptre, the jewelled ball of which was nearly as large as his head.

"I'll swallow the sceptre," he said.

"Good," cried the king, and held it toward him.

"But not now," added the Blunderer, hastily; "I'll take my time about it. You didn't say when, you know."

The kinglet turned red with rage.

"Now, by the royal Juggernaut of Jowl—" he began.

"If I should swallow it now," continued the Blunderer, calmly, "you would cease to be a kinglet; for a kinglet without a sceptre is nothing but a flibberjig."

"What!" shrieked his Majesty, jabbing the fat man furiously.

"That's right," declared Nebbie, groaning and rubbing his fat side dolefully. "A kinglet without a sceptre is a flibberjig, and I'll be black and blue by to-morrow morning!"

"Well," said his Majesty, after considering the matter, "I forbid you, Sir Blunderer, to swallow my sceptre until I give you leave."

Then his eye fell upon John Dough and Chick, who were standing at one side of the Failings, and immediately the little kinglet looked surprised, and then curious, and then annoyed. But perhaps the annoyed look was because Chick laughed in the royal face in a way that was certainly disrespectful, and even John Dough did n't look at all humble.

"Here, you Chick; behave yourself," commanded the kinglet.

"I won't," said Chick, pouting two pretty lips.

"Well, this kingdom existed at one time without an Incubator Baby, and I believe we could spare

86

you now. I'll have your saucy head cut off," declared the kinglet.

"I dare you!" said Chick, making a face.

"There's a nice child, I must say!" retorted the kinglet, scowling. "But what can we expect of a baby that has no parents and no proper bringing-up? Bah! I'm ashamed of you, Chick!"

"Don't you dare say anything against my Incubator!" cried Chick, angrily. "I guess I've had as good bringing-up as you have, you disagreeable kinglet, you!"

His Majesty was at first about to retort with equal anger; but he suddenly changed his mind and turned to John Dough.

"Who are you, stranger?" he asked. "And why are you wearing the Blunderer's armor?"

So much disrespect had been shown this kinglet by his subjects that John was about to reply lightly to these questions; but to his surprise Chick grasped his hand and whispered to him to make a low bow and to be very careful what he said. So the gingerbread man stepped forward and addressed his Majesty with great ceremony.

"Oh, most puissant and serene kinglet!" he began; "I am called John Dough, because I am made of gingerbread; and I came to your Isle because I could not help it."

The kinglet looked upon the stranger with a kindly expression.

"'Puissant and serene'!" he murmured. "Evidently, John Dough, you are a person of wit and intelligence, such as are most welcome to the Isle of Phreex. Kneel thou at my feet."

John knelt, as commanded, and the kinglet

at once dealt him a sharp blow upon the Blunderer's helmet with the heavy end of the royal sceptre. It dented in the steel plate, and would have crushed the gingerbread man's head had it not been so well protected by the helmet.

"I dub you Knight of Phreex," said his Majesty. "Rise, Sir John Dough—villain no longer, but noble and favored among my subjects!"

John stood up and bowed, although he was slightly dazed by the force of the blow.

"Long live the gentle Kinglet of Phreex," he managed to say. And Chick clapped two chubby hands with glee, and whispered: "Well done, my friend!"

"You please me, Sir John," remarked the little kinglet, swelling out his chest complacently. "I wish all the people of Phreex were so polite and discerning." Then he looked around and inquired: "Where's Sir Austed Alfrin, the Poet Laureate?"

Immediately a drapery parted, and a man with a pale, thin face and long black hair entered and saluted his Majesty with profound respect. The Poet had a bandage over one eye and hobbled as if lame in one leg. He was clothed all in black, and his long frock coat had grease spots down the front of it.

"Have you made me a sonnet to-day?" demanded the little kinglet.

"Yes, my royal Master," answered the Poet; and, pompously unrolling a scroll, he read in a loud, falsetto voice, these lines:

"There is a wise Kinglet of Phreex,
  Whose wit is so great that it leaks;
    His brain is n't big,
    But who cares a fig
  While wisdom from him fairly reeks?"

"Now, that's not so bad," said his Majesty, reflectively. "But can't you make it a little stronger, Sir Poet?"

"I'll try," replied Austed Alfrin; and after pencilling some words on his tablets he read as follows:

"The Goddess of Wisdom felt sad;
  And when asked why she whimpered so bad,
    Said: 'There's one, it is true,
    Who knows more than *I* do—
  And the Kinglet of Phreex is the lad!'"

90

"Now that," said his Majesty, "strikes me as being real poetry. How does it strike you, Sir John Dough?"

"It's fairly good," replied the gingerbread man; "but it hardly does you justice."

"The Poet does n't dare do his Majesty justice," said the Disagreeable Failing. "If he did, there would soon be no Poet."

"There's something in that, too," said the kinglet. "But now, Sir Austed, write me a sonnet on my new subject, Sir John Dough."

The Poet sighed and began writing on his tablets; and presently he read this:

"The Kinglet of Phreex, it is said,
  Has a Knight made of stale gingerbread;
    We could eat him, but yet
    The dyspepsia we'd get
  Would soon make us wish we were dead."

"That," said John, indignantly, "is rank libel; and if your Majesty will loan me your sceptre, I'll make an end of this Poet in seven seconds by the clock."

"You have my permission to make mince-meat of him," replied the kinglet, cheerfully.

"Mercy! mercy, my lord!" screamed the Poet, falling upon his knees before John and hastily wiping the verse off his tablets, "give me one more chance, I beg of you!"

"Very well," said the gingerbread knight. "But if it's no better than the last you shall be discharged. Is it not so, your Majesty?"

"Quite so," laughed the kinglet.

The Poet nervously scribbled another set of lines, which he read in a voice that trembled with fear:

> "The Gingerbread Man is so sweet,
> To eat him would be a rare treat;
> He's crisp and well spiced,
> And you'd find, were he sliced,
> That the eggs in him cannot be beat!"

"That's better," said John, "but I'm not sure about the eggs, as I did not pay much attention when I was mixed. However, this sincere tribute to my excellence will save you from my displeasure, and you may go free."

The Poet did not wait an instant, but ran from the hall as fast as his legs would carry him.

The kinglet now dismissed the Failings, who left the royal presence quarrelling and threatening one another, and making so much noise and uproar that the gingerbread man was glad to see them go.

"Are n't they nice?" asked the kinglet, looking after them. "I'd like to drown them all in the castle moat, like kittens; but every king, they say, has his Failings, so I suppose I must keep mine."

He sighed, and continued: "But what did the Poet's sonnet say about your being crisp and well spiced, and rather good eating were you sliced?"

"Don't pay any attention to that, your Majesty!" said John, hastily.

"But why not?" persisted the kinglet. "I declare, Sir John, there's something about you that makes me hungry whenever I look at you. I don't remember having eaten any gingerbread since I was a boy—ahem!—I mean since I came to rule over the Isle of Phreex. Ho there, my guards! Fetch me a knife!"

John was now trembling with terror; but Chick said to the kinglet: "Your Majesty forgets that you are to have pancakes and maple-syrup for tea. What's the use of spoiling your appetite, when you know the gingerbread man will keep good for weeks?"

"Are you sure?" asked the kinglet, anxiously. "Are you sure he'll keep? Won't he get stale?"

"Of course not," answered the child. "He's the kind of gingerbread that always keeps good. And you must n't forget he'll be a credit to the

Isle of Phreex; for whoever saw a live gingerbread man before?"

"Nobody," declared the kinglet, positively. "You're right, my Cherub; I'll save the gingerbread man for another meal, and in the mean time I can show him off before my people. We pride ourselves, Sir John, on having a greater variety of queer personages than any other kingdom in existence."

"Then you ought to be careful of them, and not permit them to be eaten," said John, still anxious. But the kinglet did not seem to hear him.

"Pancakes and maple-syrup!" muttered his Majesty, longingly. "Dear me, Chick; I wish tea were ready now."

"So do I," said Chick, laughing; for John Dough was safe from being eaten just then, whatever might be his future fate, and the child had saved him by the mention of the cakes and syrup.

But now a sudden hubbub was heard at the door, and in rushed a number of the royal guard wheeling a big platform on which was seated a woman so exceedingly fat that she appeared to be much wider than she was long.

"Here! what's the trouble with Bebe Celeste?" asked the kinglet, frowning.

BÉBÉ CELESTE

"She has lost two ounces, your Majesty," puffed one of the guards, wiping the perspiration from his forehead with his coat sleeve.

"Two ounces!" shouted the kinglet. "Now, by the toga of Samson—by the way, Nebbie, did Samson wear a toga?" He punched the fat man so severely that Nebbie gave a roar of pain before he answered.

"He wore several, your Majesty!"

"Then, by the several togas of Samson, Bebe Celeste, how dare you come before me two ounces shy?"

"I did n't come; I was brought," said the fat woman, in a wheezy voice.

"She was weighed in the balance and found wanting," said the guardsman.

"What was she wanting?" asked the kinglet.

"Two ounces, your Majesty."

The ruler rubbed his pug nose with one finger, in a reflective manner.

"Bebe," said he, "you've been exercising again. You're trying to reduce!"

The woman began to cry. "'T ain't my fault, your royal giblet—"

"Kinglet, woman!" said the fat man, without opening his eyes.

96

"Your royal kinglet, I did n't mean to lose a single flutter o' flesh. But my dog Duo got to quarrelling with himself and I got exercised in my mind—"

"Oh, the loss is in your mind, is it?" interrupted the King. "I would n't mind the loss if I had not forbidden you to exercise at all, even in your mind."

"I could n't help it, your fudgesty—"

"Majesty, woman!" said the fat man, sleepily.

"My dog Duo got to quarrelling—"

"Bring us the dog, varlets, churls, and vassals!" screeched the kinglet, in his shrill voice.

The guards stumbled over each other to obey; and presently they returned leading such a curious animal that John Dough stared at it in amazement.

It was a dog, without doubt; or rather, it was a dog's body with a head and two legs at either end of it. So that when one end walked forward the other end had to walk backward, and that made the back end growl angrily. But the same end was not always the back end of the dog; for first one head, and then the other, would prove strongest, and drag the curious animal forward.

When this double dog, which was named Duo, was brought in, both heads were snarling and

97

barking in a very noisy manner. But however much enraged they were, they could never get together to do one another mischief.

"Be silent!" yelled the kinglet, annoyed at the clamor.

But the dog's heads paid no attention to the command.

"Very well," said his Majesty; "I'll put a stop to your noise for good and all! Here, you guards, fetch me the Royal Executioner!"

The fat lady began crying anew at this, and presently the door opened and a young girl entered the hall. She was clothed in simple robes of pure white, over which her loose brown hair flowed in a soft cloud. Her eyes were large and dark and very gentle in expression, and her cheeks were fair as a lily. In one hand the maid bore a long sword, the naked blade of which shone brightly in the light. In the other hand was a sharpening-stone, and as she bowed before the kinglet she rubbed the stone gently against the keen edge of the blade.

Although the dog's heads were still quarrelling, and Bebe Celeste still weeping, it was upon John Dough that the Royal Executioner first turned her eyes.

"I hope it is n't this one, your Majesty!" she said, in a voice of disappointment; "for he won't bleed at all, being made of cake."

"I beg your pardon," exclaimed John, hastily. "I am not cake, but gingerbread."

Chick, the Cherub

"It's just the same," she answered, sighing; "you would n't bleed if I cut you into bits."

"Why are you so bloodthirsty?" asked John, looking reproachfully into the girl's gentle eyes.

"Because I'm the Royal Executioner, I suppose," she answered. "I've held the office ever since my father was destroyed by an earthquake; but I've never yet executed a single person. The kinglet calls me in about a dozen times a day, but something always happens to rob me of my victim. I've worn out three sword blades, sharpening them, but I've never carved anything yet!"

"Be of good cheer," said his Majesty, "for now you shall see blood flow like water. This time I am fully resolved to be terrible. Cut me this snarling cur into two parts!"

"What, the dog?" asked the girl, surprised. And Bebe began to scream loudly; and the fat man woke  up and shook his head, and Chick patted both heads of the animal tenderly, and a guardsman cried out: "Oh, no, your Majesty!"

"And why not?" inquired the kinglet.

"Why, this is the most valuable creature in all your dominions!" said the guard. "Do you desire to rob yourself of such a treasure, your Majesty?"

The kinglet hesitated, and then jabbed the fat man with his sceptre.

"Is it so, Nebbie?" he asked.

"It is so, my Lord," answered the fat man. "If you want to butcher anything, cut up a few of the Royal Guards, or mince the Failings, or carve Chick, the Cherub. But the dog Duo is one of the remarkable features of your kingdom, and should be preserved at all hazards. Why, he's worth more than Bebe Celeste."

"That reminds me of Bebe," said the kinglet, looking at the fat one sternly. "Take her away, guards, and stuff her with mashed potatoes and pate de foi gras. If she doesn't regain those two ounces in three days, she'll disgrace my kingdom, and I'll turn her over to the Royal Executioner."

So the guards trundled away the platform on which the fat lady sat, and the dog Duo followed, first one head leading, and then the other. And now his Majesty threw off his ermine robe and laid down the sceptre and scrambled out of the throne.

"The royal audience is ended for to-day," he said, "and now I'll go and see if those cakes and maple-syrup are ready for tea. And see here, you Incubator Baby, look after Sir John Dough, and mind that nobody eats him. If there's one bite gone when I see him again I'll turn you over to the Royal Executioner——and then there won't be any Incubator Baby."

Then his Majesty walked away, chuckling to himself in a very disagreeable manner. At once the fat Nebbie rolled out of his low seat and stood up, yawning and stretching out his arms.

"Our kinglet is a hard master," said he, with a sigh, "and I really wish some one would get up a revolution and dethrone him. He's been punching my ribs all day long, and I'll be black and blue by to-morrow morning."

102

"He's cruel," said Chick, patting the fat man's hand, as if to comfort him.

"Yet he's too tender-hearted to suit me," complained the lovely Executioner. "If I could only shed a single drop of blood, I'd feel that I am of some use in the world."

"How dreadful!" cried John, with a shudder.

"Oh, not at all!" said the girl. "For what's the object of being an Executioner if one can't execute?" And she tucked the sword under her arm and took out her handkerchief and went away weeping sorrowfully.

The Freaks of Phreex

"Well, did n't I take care of you all right?" laughed the Incubator Baby, leading John Dough from the throne-room and up a broad flight of marble stairs.

"Indeed you did," he answered, gratefully. "Really, my dear Chick, I believe that dreadful kinglet would have eaten me but for you."

"'Course he would," said the Cherub, nodding gayly; "and won't he be wild when he finds there are no pancakes and maple-syrup for tea?"

John stopped short. "Are n't there?" he asked. "Oh, Chick! I'm afraid he'll punish you for deceiving him."

"I don't mind," declared the child. "No one shall eat a friend of mine that I've given my promise to take care of. So come along, John Dough, and don't worry. I've got a lovely room on the top floor of this castle, and I'll share it with you."

104

So John mounted more marble steps, until finally Chick brought him to a handsome apartment on the third story.

105

"Here we are!" cried the Baby. "Now, make yourself at home, John, for we need n't fear the kinglet until to-morrow morning, and then he'll have forgotten that I fooled him."

Our hero's first act was to take off the Blunderer's heavy armor and pile it in one corner of the room. When free from the weight of metal he felt more like himself again, and walked to the window to view the scenery.

"It's a pretty place, Chick," he remarked.

"Oh, the Isle is all right," answered the child. "It's the people here that are all wrong, as you'll soon find out. Do you ever eat, John Dough?"

"Never," said John.

"Then, while you're waiting here, I'll go over to the dairy and get my milk for tea. You don't mind if I leave you for a few minutes, do you?"

"Not at all," he declared. "But it has just started to rain, outside; you'll get wet, won't you?"

"That's nothing," laughed Chick. "I won't melt."

"It's different with me," said John, sadly. "If my gingerbread body got soaked it would fall to pieces."

That made the little one laugh again, and it ran merrily from the room and left John Dough alone

"HELLO, NEIGHBOR"

to stare out of the window. There was a projecting cornice overhead, so he had pushed his head well out to observe the pretty scenery, when suddenly he heard a voice say, in a tone of astonishment:

"Hello, neighbor!"

Turning toward the left, he saw sticking out of the next window to his own a long bald head that slanted up to a peak, underneath which appeared a little withered face that was smiling in a most friendly manner.

John bowed politely.

"Well, well," said the owner of the bald head. "Here's another curiosity come to our island! Wait a minute, and I'll run in and make your acquaintance." So presently the bald head, which was perched upon the body of a little, dried-up looking man, entered John's room and bowed politely.

"I'm Sir Pryse Bocks," he said, "and the remarkable thing about me is that I'm an inventor, and a successful one. You, I perceive, are a delicatessen; a friend in knead; I might say, a Pan-American. Ha, ha!"

"Pleased to make your acquaintance," returned John, bowing. "But do not joke about my person, Sir Pryse. I'm proud of it."

"I respect your pride, sir," said the other. "It's bread in the bone, doubtless. Ha, ha!"

John looked at him reproachfully, and the little man at once grew grave.

"This island is full of inventors," said he; "but they're all cranks, and don't amount to anything — except me."

"What have you invented?" asked John.

"This!" said the other, taking a little tube from his pocket. "You will notice that it often rains — it's raining now, if you'll look outside. And the reason it rains is because the drops of water fall to the earth by the attraction of gravitation."

"I suppose so," said John.

"Now, what do people usually do when it rains?" asked the little man.

"They grumble," said John.

"Yes, and they use umbrellas — *umbrellas*, mind you, to keep themselves dry!"

"And that is quite sensible," declared John.

The bald-headed one gave a scornful laugh. "It's ridiculous!" he said, angrily. "An umbrella is a big, clumsy thing, that the wind jerks out of your hand, or turns inside out; and it's a nuisance to carry it around; and people always borrow it and never bring it back. An umbrella, sir, is a humbug! A relic of the Dark Ages! I've done away with the use of umbrellas entirely, by means of this invention — this little tube, which can be carried in one's pocket!"

He held up a small instrument that looked like a tin whistle.

"How curious!" said John.

"Isn't it? You see, within this tube is stored a Power of Repulsion that overcomes the Attraction of Gravitation, and sends the rain-drops flying upward again. You stick the tube in your hat-band and walk out boldly into the rain. Immediately all the rain-drops shoot up into the air, and before they can fall again you have passed on! It's always dry where the wearer of this tube goes, for it protects him perfectly. And when it stops raining, you put it in your pocket again and it's all ready for another time. Isn't it great, sir? Isn't it wonderful? Isn't the inventor of this tube the greatest man in the world?"

"I'd like to try it," said John, "for no one needs protection from the rain more than I do. Being made of gingerbread, it would ruin me to get wet."

"True," agreed the other. "I'll lend you the tube, with pleasure. Stick it in your hat-band."

"I have no hat," said John; and then he remembered that he had left both the baker's hat and his candy cane lying on the sands where he had first fallen.

"Well, carry the tube in your hand, then," said the inventor. "It will work just as well that way, but it's not so convenient."

So John took the tube; and having thanked the bald-headed man for his kindness, he left the room and walked down the stairs and through the big, empty hall, and so out into the courtyard.

The rain seemed to have driven every one in doors, for not a person could he see.

Holding the tube upright, he boldly walked into the rain; and it gave him great pleasure to notice that not a drop fell near him. Indeed, by looking upward, he could see the falling drops stop short and then fly toward the clouds; and he began to believe that the bald-headed inventor was really as great a man as he claimed to be.

After descending the slippery path through the rocks, he crossed the patch of green, and at last reached the sandy shore, where he found the baker's hat, soaked through by the rain. As he lifted it he saw the crooked handle of the candy cane sticking out of the sand, and drew it forth to find it in excellent condition, little of the dampness having reached it.

But now, as John Dough began to retrace his steps, he discovered that his feet were soft and swollen. For he had been walking on the damp ground and through the wet grass; and although no rain had fallen upon his body, his feet were getting to be in a dangerous condition, and the licorice in them had become sticky. After he had recrossed the grass and come to the edge of the rocks he began to be frightened, for bits of his left heel now commenced to crumble and drop in the path; and when he tried walking on his flabby toes, they were so soggy and soft that he knew they would not last very long.

While he paused, bewildered, another calamity overtook him. For the tube suddenly lost its power of repulsion and ceased to work, and the raindrops began to pelt his unprotected body and sink into his flesh. He looked around with a groan of dismay, and discovered a round hole, or tunnel, in the rock near by. Staggering toward this, he entered the tunnel and found that now no rain could reach him. The floor was smooth and dry, and in the far distance he saw a light twinkling.

Not daring to walk farther upon his mushy feet, John got down on his hands and knees and began crawling toward the farther end of the tunnel. He made slow progress, in that position; but soon he heard a noise of machinery, and felt the warm air of a furnace coming to meet him. That gave him courage to proceed, and he crawled onward until he had reached a large, circular chamber, where a tall man with whiskers that resembled those of a billy-goat was busily working among a number of machines.

"Hello!" this personage exclaimed, as he saw the gingerbread man. "What have we here?"

The voice and eyes were alike kindly; so John told the man his story and asked permission to dry his feet at the glowing furnace.

"Make yourself at home," said the man, and turned to his work again.

The place was lighted by electricity, and was

warm and comfortable. John put his feet as near
to the furnace as he dared, and soon felt the heat
drying up his soaked feet. It was not long, indeed,
before his entire body was as crisp and solid as ever;
and then our hero stood upon his feet and found
that the damage to his heel would not interfere
much with his walking.

"What are you doing?" he asked the man.

"Making diamonds," replied the other, calmly.
"I suppose I am the only one in the world who ever

succeeded in making real diamonds; but people did not believe in me, you see, so they sent me to the Isle of Phreex. Here I have manufactured the finest diamonds the world has ever known, for no one interferes with my work. Look at these."

He threw back the lid of a large tin box, and John saw that it was full to the brim with sparkling gems of a clear white color.

"Take some," said the man, offering him a handful. "They are of no use to me here, because I cannot dispose of them. But I have the satisfaction of making them, just the same. Help yourself!"

"No, thank you," said John. "I have no use for diamonds, any more than you have."

"But the time may come when riches will be a great help to you," said the man, and picking out three very big stones he began pressing them into John Dough's gingerbread body, one after the other.

"There!" he exclaimed. "They are now safely concealed, and if you ever need them you can dig them out and sell them. Those three stones would be worth several thousand dollars if you ever get into the world again, where diamonds are valued."

"You are very generous," said John.

"Oh, not at all, I assure you!" said the man, wagging his goatlike beard with every word he spoke. "In this curious island there is no value to anything whatever, not even to life. All I can do with my diamonds here is to stick them into the kinglet's crown and sceptre; so I'm getting a big stock of them laid by. Very soon I shall begin studding the roof of the throne-room with diamonds, and it will be a pretty sight to see them glittering in one mass."

"Well, said our hero, "if it has stopped raining, I believe I'll bid you good-by."

"Never mind the rain," answered the man. "Here is a winding staircase that leads directly upward into the castle. If you go that way, the rain cannot reach you. The tunnel through which you entered is only used for ventilation."

John thanked the good-natured diamond-maker and started to climb the stairs. There were a good many steps, but after a while he came to a gallery of the castle, and had little difficulty in finding the passage that led to his own room.

As he walked along he heard the sound of a piano, and paused at an open door to peer within the room, for he imagined some one was pounding upon the keys of the piano with a sledge-hammer.

116

THE MUSICIAN THREW HIMSELF UPON THE PIANO

117

But immediately a fluffy-haired man looked up and saw him, and the next instant pounced upon the gingerbread man in much the same way that a cat would pounce upon a rat, and seized him fast, drew him into the room, and closed and locked the door.

John was astonished, but the fluffy-haired musician began pacing up and down the room, swinging his arms and shouting:

"I have it! I have it at last! I am great! I am magnificent! I am better than Vogner himself!" He paused to glare upon John. "Why don't you shout, you baked idiot? Why don't you weep with joy?" he cried. "It is great, I tell you! It is great!"

"What is great?" asked John.

"The symphonie! The divine symphonie, you heartless molasses-cake, or devil's food, or whatever you are! And I composed it—*I*—Tietjamus Toips! I am greater than Vogner!"

"I didn't hear it," said the gingerbread man.

The musician threw himself upon the piano, and produced a succession of such remarkable sounds that John was surprised.

"Did you understand it?" demanded the fluffy-haired one, jumping up again.

"No," said John.

"No! Of course not! No one can understand it. It is genius! It will be played at all the great concerts. The critics will write columns in praise of it. Some folks can understand Vogner a little. No one can understand *me* at all! I am wonderful! I am superb!"

"Well," said John, "I'm not a judge. It seemed to me like awful discord."

The musician threw himself upon his knees and burst into tears.

"Thank you, my friend!—my *dear* friend!" said he, between the sobs. "Such praise gladdens my heart and makes me very happy! Ah! glorious moment, in which I produce music that is not understood and sounds like discord!"

John left the musician still shedding tears of happiness, and walked to his room.

"The people of this island are certainly peculiar," he reflected; "and I am very glad indeed that I am an ordinary gingerbread man, and not a crank."

He found the bald-headed inventor of the power of repulsion awaiting him in the room.

"Well, how did the tube please you? Is it not wonderful?" he inquired.

"It's wonderful enough when it works," said

John; "but it suddenly quit working, and nearly ruined me."

"Ah, the power became exhausted," returned the man, calmly, "But that is nothing. It can be easily renewed."

"However," John remarked, "I think that whenever any one uses your tube as a protection from the rain, he should also carry an umbrella to use in case of accident."

"An umbrella! Bah!" cried the inventor, and left the room in a rage, slamming the door behind him.

The Lady Executioner

Presently Chick returned, looking bright and happy as ever; but when the child heard the tale of John's wanderings in the rain he received a sound scolding for being so careless.

"You must n't pay any attention to the inventors," said the Cherub. "This Isle is full of 'em, and most of their inventions won't work."

"I 've discovered that," said John.

"But they 're good fun, if you don't take 'em in earnest," continued the Baby; "and as it 's going to rain all the afternoon I 'll take you around the castle to make some calls on some of the cranks that are harmless.

John readily agreed to this proposal; so Chick took his hand and led him through some of the wide halls, stopping frequently to call upon the different inventors and scientific discoverers who inhabited the various rooms. They were all glad to see the pretty child and welcomed John Dough almost as cordially.

The Lady Executioner

One personage presented the gingerbread man with a smokeless cigar that he had recently invented. Another wanted him to listen to a noisless music-box, and was delighted when John declared he could hear nothing at all. A third wanted him to try a dish of hot ice-cream made in a glowing freezer, and was grieved because the gingerbread man was constructed in such a way that it was impossible for him to eat.

"Really," said John, "I don't see the use of these things."

"Oh, they're not useful at all," replied Chick, laughing; "but these folks are all trying to do something queer, and most of them are doing it. Now we'll climb this tower, and I'll show you what I call a really fine invention."

So up they climbed to the top of one of the turrets, winding round and round a narrow staircase until they came upon a broad platform. And on this platform rested a queer machine that somewhat resembled a bird, for it had two great wings and a big body that glittered as brightly as if it were made of silver.

While they stood looking at this odd contrivance a door in the body of the bird opened and a young man stepped out and greeted them.

"THIS IS IMAR," SAID CHICK

123

The Lady Executioner

John thought him quite the most agreeable person, in looks and manner, that he had yet met in the Isle of Phreex; excepting, of course, his friend Chick. The young man had a sad face, but his eyes were pleasant and intelligent and his brow thoughtful. In a few polite and well-chosen words he welcomed his guests.

"This is Imar," said Chick, introducing John; "and he has invented a real flying-machine."

"One that will fly?" asked John, curiously.

"Of course," said the Baby. "I've had many a ride in it—have n't I, Imar?"

"To be sure," replied the young man. "I have often taken Chick to ride as far as forty yards from the tower. If it did not rain, just now, nothing would give me more pleasure than to prove to you that my invention will work perfectly."

"I see you have made it resemble a bird," remarked John, who was quite interested in the machine.

"Yes," said the dreamy Imar, "and the reason I have succeeded in my invention is because I have kept close to Nature's own design. Every muscle of a bird's wings is duplicated in this machine. But instead of being animated by life, I have found it necessary to employ electric batteries and motors.

124

Perhaps the bird is n't exactly as good as a real bird, but it will fly all right, as you shall see when I take you for a ride in it."

He then allowed John to enter the tiny room in the body of the bird, which was just big enough to allow two to sit close together. And in front of the seat were various push-buttons and a silver lever, by means of which the flight of the machine was controlled.

"It is very simple," said Imar, proudly. "Even Chick could guide the machine, if properly instructed. The only fault of the invention is that the wings are too light to be strong, and that is why I do not take very long trips in it."

"I understand," answered John. "It's quite a distance to the ground, if anything happened to break."

"True," acknowledged Imar, sadly; "and I do not wish to break my neck before I am able to make a bigger and better machine."

"That is not to be wondered at," said John. Then he thanked the inventor and followed Chick down the winding stairs and through the halls until they again reached their own room, where they sat and talked until darkness came and drove the Incubator Baby to its snowy couch. As for the gingerbread man, he never required sleep or rest; so he sat quietly in a chair and thought of many things until a new day dawned.

By morning the rain had ceased and the sun arose in a blue sky and flooded the Isle with its warm and brilliant rays. The Incubator Baby was so happy this pleasant day that it fairly danced away to get its regular breakfast of milk and oatmeal.

But John Dough's little friend was back at his side before long, and together they went hand in hand through the halls of the castle to the throne-room of the kinglet.

They found his Majesty already seated in the throne, with the fat Nebbie asleep at one side of him and the girl executioner carefully sharpening her sword on the other side.

"This is my busy day," said the kinglet, nodding graciously to Chick and the gingerbread man. "There are too many useless people in my kingdom, and I 'm going to kill off some of them. Sit down and watch the flash of the executioner's sword."

Then he turned to his guards and commanded: "Bring in the General."

Immediately they ushered before the kinglet a soldierly man clothed in a gorgeous uniform. His head was erect and his countenance calm and set. The eyes seemed dull and listless, and he walked stiffly, as if his limbs were rheumatic.

"Sire, I salute you!" the General exclaimed, in a hollow voice. "Why am I brought before you as a prisoner—I, the hero of a hundred battles?"

"You are accused of being foolish," said the kinglet, with a broad grin upon his freckled face.

"Sire, at the battle of Waterloo—"

"Never mind the battle of Waterloo," interrupted his Majesty. "I am told you are scattered all over the world, as the result of your foolishness."

"To an extent, Sire, I am scattered. But it is the result of bravery, not foolishness." He unstrapped his left arm and tossed it on the floor before the throne. "I lost that at Bull Run," he said. Then he unhooked his right leg

127

and cast it down. "That, Sire, was blown off at Sedan." Then he suddenly lifted his right arm, seized his hair firmly, and lifted the head from his shoulders. "It is true I lost my head at Santiago," he said, "but I could not help it."

John was astonished. The old general seemed to come to pieces very easily. He had tucked the head under his right elbow, and now stood before the kinglet on one foot, presenting a remarkably strange appearance.

His Majesty seemed interested.

"What is your head made of?" he asked.

"Wax, your Majesty."

"And what are your legs made of?" continued the kinglet.

"One is cork, Sire, and the other—the one I am now standing on—is basswood."

"And your arms?"

"Rubber, my kinglet."

"You may go, General. There is no doubt you were very unwise to get so broken up; but there is nothing left for the Royal Executioner to do."

The girl sighed and felt the edge of her blade; and the old general replaced his head, had his leg and arm again strapped to his body by the

guards, and hobbled away after making a low bow
before the throne.

Just then a great noise of quarrelling and fighting was heard near the doorway, and while all eyes
were turned toward the sound, a wooden Indian

sprang into the hall, waving a wooden tomahawk
over his head, and uttering terrible war-whoops.

Following him came a number of the Brotherhood of Failings, trying to capture the Indian.

The Lady Executioner

The Awkward tripped up and fell flat on his face; the Unlucky got in the way of the tomahawk and received a crack on the head that laid him low; the Blunderer was kicked on the shin so violently that he howled and limped away to a safe distance. But just before the throne the Disagreeable, the Bad-Tempered, and the Ugly managed to throw a rope about the Indian's arms and bind them fast to his body, so that he ceased to struggle.

"What's the trouble?" asked the kinglet.

"Sir," said the Indian, proudly; "once I had the honor to be a beautiful sign in front of a cigar store, and now these miserable Failings dare to insult me."

"He claims his name is Wart-on-the-Nose," answered the Disagreeable, "and any one can see there is no wart at all on his nose."

"So we decided to fight him," added the Ugly.

"And he dared to resist," said the Bad-Tempered.

"I am a great chief," the Indian declared, scowling fiercely. "I am made of oak, and my paint is the best ready-mixed that can be purchased!"

"But why do you claim your name is Wart-on-the-Nose?" asked the kinglet.

"I have a right to call myself what I please," answered the Indian, sulkily. "Are not white girls called Rose and Violet when they have not that color? John Brown was white and Mary Green was white. If the white people deceive us about their names, I also have a right to deceive."

"Now, by my — my — my —" The kinglet jabbed the fat man with his sceptre.

"Halidom!" yelled Nebbie, with a jump.

"By my halidom!" said the kinglet, "I will allow no one in my kingdom to tell an untruth. There being no wart on your nose, you must die the death! Executioner, do your duty!"

The Failings tripped up the Indian so that he fell upon his face, and then the girl advanced solemnly with her sword.

Three times she swung the glittering blade around her head, and then she glanced at the kinglet and said:

"Well!"

"Well, what?" asked his Majesty.

"Isn't it time to change your mind?"

"I'm not going to change my mind in this case," said the kinglet. "Chop off his head!"

At this the girl screamed and drew back.

"Do you really mean it?"

"Of course."

"Oh, your Majesty, I couldn't hurt the poor

thing!" sobbed the Executioner. "It would be simply awful! *Please* change your mind, as you always have done."

"I won't," said the kinglet, sternly. "You do as I tell you, Maria Simpson, or I'll have *you* executed next!"

The girl hesitated. Then she took the sword in both her hands, shut her eyes, and struck downward with all her might. The blade fell upon the Indian's neck and shivered into several pieces.

"He's wood, your Majesty," said the Executioner. "I simply *can't* cut his head off."

"Get a meat cleaver!" cried the kinglet. "Do you suppose I'll allow Wart-on-the-Nose to live

132

when he has n't any wart on his nose? Get the cleaver instantly!"

So the girl brought a big meat cleaver, and lifting it high in the air, struck the Indian's neck as hard as she could.

The cleaver stuck fast in the wood; but it did n't cut far enough to do much harm to the victim. Indeed, Wart-on-the-Nose even laughed, and then he said:

"There's a knot in that neck—a good oak knot. You could n't chop my head off in a thousand years!"

The kinglet was annoyed.

"Pull out that cleaver," he commanded.

The girl tried to obey, but the cleaver stuck fast. Then the Failings tried, one after another; but it would n't budge.

"Never mind, leave it there," said the Indian, rolling over and then getting upon his feet. "It won't bother me in the least. In fact, it will make a curious ornament."

"Look here, Sir John Dough," said the kinglet, turning to the gingerbread man; "what am I going to do? I 've said the Indian must die, because he has no wart on his nose. And I find I can't kill him. Now, you must either tell me how to get out of this scrape or I'll cut *your* head off! And it won't be as hard to cut gingerbread as it is wood, I promise you."

This speech rather frightened John, for he knew he was in great danger. But after thinking a moment he replied:

"Why, it seems to me very easy to get out of the difficulty, your Majesty. The Indian's only offense is that he has no wart on his nose."

"But that is a great offense!" cried the kinglet.

"Well, let us whittle a wart on his nose," said John, "and then all will be well."

The kinglet looked at him in astonishment.

"Can that be done?" he asked.

"Certainly, your Majesty. It is only necessary to carve away some of the wood of his nose, and leave a wart."

"I'll do it!" shouted the kinglet, in great delight.

And he at once sent for the Royal Carpenter and had the man whittle the Indian's nose until a beautiful wart showed plainly on the very end.

"Good!" said the King.

"Good!" echoed the Indian, proudly. "Now none of those miserable Failings dare say my name is not suitable!"

"I'm very sorry about that cleaver," remarked the kinglet. "You'll have to carry it around wherever you go."

"That's all right. I'll add to my name and call myself Wart-on-the-Nose-and-Cleaver-in-the-Neck. That will be a fine Indian name, and no one can prove it is not correct."

Saying this, the wooden Indian bowed to the kinglet, gave a furious war-whoop, and stalked stiffly from the room.

"Bring on the next prisoner!" shouted the kinglet, and both Chick and John gave a gasp of surprise as Imar was brought into the room. The inventor of the flying-machine, however, did not seem the least bit frightened, and bowed calmly before the throne.

"What's the charge against this man?" inquired the kinglet.

"He's accused of being a successful inventor," said one of the guards. "The other inventors claim no one who succeeds has a right to live in the Isle of Phreex."

"Quite correct," replied his Majesty. "Cut off his head, Maria."

"Alas, Sire! my sword is broken!" she exclaimed.

"Then get another."

"But I have no other sword that is sharpened," she protested.

"Then sharpen one!" retorted the kinglet, frowning.

"Certainly, your Majesty. But a sword cannot be properly sharpened in a minute. It will take until to-morrow, at least, to get it ready."

"Then," said the kinglet, "I'll postpone the execution until to-morrow morning at nine o'clock. "If you're not ready by that time I'll get a new Royal Executioner and you'll lose your job."

"I shall be ready," said the girl, and walked away arm in arm with the sad young man, on whom she smiled sweetly.

"It's all right," whispered Chick to John. "Imar won't get hurt, for the kinglet will forget all about him by to-morrow."

"And now, my guards," said his Majesty, stretching his arms and yawning, "bring hither my two-legged horse, that I may take a ride around my kingdom."

So presently the guards led in a big, raw-boned nag that had two legs instead of four, and these

"NOW, YOU SIT STILL AND BEHAVE YOURSELF"

137

two set in the middle of its body. It seemed rather frisky and pranced around in a nervous manner, so that the kinglet had great difficulty in mounting the horse's back, whereon was a saddle made of purple velvet and cloth of gold.

"Hold still, can't you?" cried the kinglet.

"I can; but I won't," said the horse, in a cross tone, for it appeared the animal was able to talk.

"I'll thrash you soundly, if you don't behave!" screamed the kinglet.

"I'll kick you in the ribs, if you dare to threaten me!" returned the horse, laying back its ears. "Why, you miserable little freckle-faced kinglet, I could run away with you and break your neck, if I wanted to!"

"That's true," said his Majesty, meekly "I beg your pardon for my harsh words. Let us be friends, by all means!"

The horse snorted, as if with contempt, and the guards finally managed to hoist the little kinglet to his seat upon the animal's back.

"Throw away that mace!" cried the horse.

His Mayesty obeyed, at once.

"Now," said the animal, "you sit still and behave yourself, or I'll dump you over my head. Understand?"

The Lady Executioner

"I understand," said the kinglet.

"Very good!" declared the horse. "When you 're on your throne you 're a tyrant; but when you 're on horseback you 're a coward, because you 're at my mercy, and you know it. Now, we are off."

The beast pranced down the hall and out of the arched entrance, bearing the kinglet upon his back; and when they were gone John and Chick started to take a walk along the beach of the seashore.

But no sooner had they stepped into the court-yard than an awful yell saluted their ears, and before them stood the form of the terrible Arab!

The Palace of Romance

"He must have broken loose!" cried Chick. "Let us run, John Dough, before he can eat you."

At once John turned to fly, with Chick grasping his hand to urge him on. Ali Dubh had indeed succeeded in breaking through the iron grating of his prison, and had even managed to untie his hands. But his legs were still firmly bound together from his ankles to his knees, so that he could only move toward them by hopping.

Nevertheless, at sight of the gingerbread man, who was mixed with his precious Elixir, the Arab began bounding toward his victim with long hops, and had John and Chick not run so fast as they did it is certain the Arab would soon have overtaken them. Through the throne-room they fled, with Ali Dubh just behind them, and then they

140

"HURRY, JOHN DOUGH, OR YOU'LL BE EATEN!"

began mounting the marble stairways to the upper stories of the castle.

Their pursuer, nothing daunted by his bound legs, hopped up the stairs after them with remarkable swiftness.

"Hurry!" cried Chick; "hurry, John Dough, or you'll be eaten."

They came to the second flight of stairs, and still the Arab followed.

"We are lost," said John, in despair. "He'll surely get me this time."

But Chick tugged at his puffy brown hand and hurried him on, for the Incubator Baby at that very moment thought of a clever way to save the gingerbread man. Still holding John's hand, the child ran through the upper passages to the foot of the tower of Imar, and began climbing up the steep stairs as fast as possible. Luckily for the fugitives, these stairs to the tower were very difficult for Ali Dubh to climb by hopping. When he was half-way up he lost his balance and tumbled down again, and this accident gave John and Chick time to enter the body of the bird flying-machine, which still lay stretched upon the roof of the tower.

"Quick!" shouted the child, shutting and fastening the silver door behind them. "Pull over that lever, and away we go!"

"Is it safe?" asked John, hesitating.

"Is it safe to be eaten?" inquired Chick.

John quickly grabbed the lever, pulled it over, and the hugh bird fluttered its wings once or twice and rose slowly into the air. It sailed away from the roof just as the Arab appeared at the top of the stairs.

"Stop!" screamed Ali Dubh. "You're mine, John Dough. Come back and be eaten."

"Don't mind him," said the Cherub, peeping at the Arab through a little window in the bottom of the bird's body. "And don't worry about this flying-machine, either. Imar has told me how to run it, and it will carry us somewhere, never fear. This button that I pushed is to start it, and there's another button somewhere to stop it."

"Where?" asked John.

"I don't remember. But never mind that; we don't want to stop just yet, anyhow."

John stooped to look through the little window, and saw spread out beneath him the Isle of Phreex. The Brotherhood of Failings stood upon the shore watching the flight of the machine, and the kinglet was riding along calmly upon his two-legged horse without any idea that the Incubator Baby and the gingerbread man were leaving his kingdom for good and all and he would probably never see them again.

The great bird flew steadily westward, and Chick laughed and chatted, and seemed to enjoy the journey immensely. They were flying over the ocean now, and before long the Isle they had left became a mere speck upon the water.

"Where are we going?" John asked.

"I don't know," answered Chick.

"What land lies in this direction?"

"I haven't the faintest idea," said the Baby.

John became thoughtful.

"How long will this machine fly?" he inquired.

"Who knows?" said Chick. "Imar was always afraid to go very far from the island with it. We'll just have to wait and find out."

This was not very encouraging, but it was too late to return now, the Isle of Phreex being lost in the vastness of the great sea. Moreover, John reflected that he would be in greater danger there from Ali Dubh than in riding in an untried flying-machine. The only thing to do was to continue the flight through the air until they sighted some other land—provided the machine did not suddenly break down. It seemed to be all right just at present, and John's admiration of Imar's genius in constructing it grew steadily as the bird flopped on and on without a sign of giving out.

Chick wasn't frightened, that was certain. The Baby laughed and sang little songs, and seemed as

145

The Palace of Romance

happy and contented as when upon firm land; so John gradually forgot his fears. The sun had sank low upon the horizon, and was looking for a good place to dive into the sea, when the voyagers discovered something far ahead of them that glittered brightly upon the water. Neither could determine what the glitter meant, until they drew nearer and saw a small, rocky islet, upon which was perched an enormous palace that seemed to be made of pure gold, having many crystal windows set in its domes and sides.

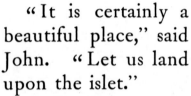

"It is certainly a beautiful place," said John. "Let us land upon the islet."

"All right," returned Chick. "I'll see if I can find out which button stops the thing."

The Baby pushed one of the buttons, and at once the bird shot up higher into the air.

"That isn't it!" cried John, in sudden alarm.

Chick pushed another button, and the machine began whirling around in short circles.

"Dear me!" said John; "what's going to happen to us?"

Chick laughed and pushed another button.

"One of 'em *must* be to stop," declared Chick, cheerfully; "and there's only two more left."

The bird paused, with a quick trembling of its wings, and slowly fluttered downward.

"Oh, now we're all right," gayly announced the queer child, "for there's only one button left; and when I push it, John Dough, you must pull back the silver lever and steer straight for the golden palace."

Down, down they sank, and fortunately the descent was made to the flat roof of a wing of the palace. When they had almost reached it, Chick, who was watching the roof through the little window, pushed the last button, while John threw over the lever.

Immediately the flying-machine fell with a thump that made the gingerbread man's candy teeth knock together.

"Wow!" said Chick. "That was a jolt and a half! I hope nothing's broken."

The Palace of Romance

"I don't believe I will ever ride in it again," said John, smoothing the wrinkles out of his frosted shirt-front and pulling the baker's hat off his eyes, where it had become jammed. "These air-ships are too dangerous to suit me."

"Why, the bird has saved your life, and it may save it again," said Chick. "For my part, I rather like flying through the air. You never know what's going to happen next. And see how lucky we are! This is the only part of the palace roof that is flat, and we struck it to a dot. If we'd fallen upon one of those spikes"— pointing to the numerous spires and minarets— "our clocks would have stopped by this time."

"You have a queer way of expressing yourself, my friend," said John, looking upon the child gravely. "The vast knowledge I gained by means of the Elixir taught me nothing of your methods of twisting language."

"That's too bad," answered Chick. "I can't always figure out what you mean to say; but you always know what I mean, don't you?"

"Almost always," John acknowledged.

"Then don't kick," said the Baby, sweetly; and the gingerbread man looked at his feet with a

CHICK DISCOVERS A TRAP DOOR   149

puzzled expression, and then back into the child's smiling face, and sighed.

By this time they had climbed out of the bird's body and stood upon the roof. It was so high above the rocks that it made John dizzy to look down; but Chick soon discovered a trap-door that led downward into the palace by means of a tiny staircase. They descended the stairs, and, having pushed aside a heavy drapery that hung across a doorway, came upon a broad passage running through the upper story of the palace. This led to still another passage, and still another; but although they turned this way and that in the maze of passages, no living person did they meet with. The tiled floors and paneled walls were very beautiful and splendid; but they were so much alike that our adventurers completely lost their way before they came by accident to a broad staircase leading downward to the next story. These stairs were covered with soft carpeting and the balusters were of filigree gold. Still no one was to be seen either on the stairs or in the passages, and the palace was silent as could be.

They found another staircase, by and by, and descended to the main floor of the palace, passing through magnificent parlors and galleries, until finally a hum of pleasant voices reached their ears.

"I feel much relieved," said John, "for I had begun to think the place was uninhabited."

"Let us go on," replied Chick, "and see who these people are."

Turning first to the right and then to left, and now following a high-arched marble passage, the adventurers suddenly found themselves before heavy draperies of crimson velvet, from beyond which came clearly the sounds of laughter and the merry chattering of many people.

They pushed aside the draperies and entered a splendid domed chamber of such exquisite beauty that the sight made even Chick pause in astonishment.

All around the sides and in the ceiling were set handsome windows made of bits of colored glass, so arranged that they formed very pleasing pictures. Between the windows were panels of wrought gold having many brilliant gems set in the metal. The floor was covered with priceless rugs of quaint patterns, and the furniture consisted of many settees and easy-chairs designed to offord the highest degree of comfort.

Fountains of perfumed waters sparkled here and

there, falling into golden basins; and little tables scattered about the room bore trays of dainty refreshments.

Seated within the room were groups of ladies and gentlemen, all clothed in gorgeous apparel, soft

of speech, graceful and courteous in demeanor, and with kindly faces.

These looked up with joyous surprise as the gingerbread man and Chick entered, and the gentlemen all arose and bowed politely to the strangers.

"Welcome!" cried the ladies, in a soft chorus; and then two of their number came forward and led their unexpected guests to seats in the very center of the room. Others offered them refreshment, of which Chick eagerly partook, for the child was hungry. John Dough was obliged to explain that he did not eat, and they accepted his speech very graciously and did not remark at all upon his unusual personality.

When the child had finished eating, John said:

"May I ask what palace this is, and who rules upon this island?"

The ladies and gentlemen exchanged significant looks, and smiled; but one made answer, in a deferential voice:

"Good sir, this is the Palace of Romance; and we have no ruler at all, each one of our number having equal power and authority with the others."

"We pass our time," said another, "in telling of tales of romance and adventure; and, whenever a stranger comes to our palace, we require him to amuse us by telling all the stories he may know."

"That is a fair requirement," replied John. "I think I shall like this Palace of Romance, although I do not know many tales."

"The more tales you know the longer you may enjoy our palace," one of the ladies remarked, earnestly.

153

The Palace of Romance

"How is that?" asked John, surprised.

They were silent for a time, and ceased laughing. But finally one of the gentlemen said:

"Our laws oblige us to destroy every stranger, after he has related to us all the stories he knows.

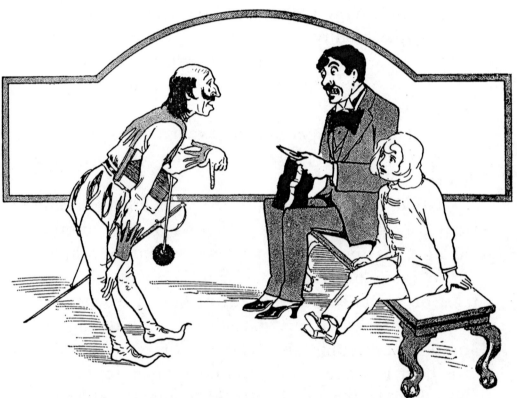

It grieves us very much to tell you this; but the laws cannot be changed, and the death is very simple and without much pain. For you will be dropped through a trap into a long slide leading to the bottom of the sea; and it is said there is little discomfort in drowning."

Now, at this John looked pale and worried, and even the laughing Chick became thoughtful. Several of the ladies wiped their eyes with delicate handkerchiefs, as if in sorrow for their fate, and the men all sighed sympathetically.

"Why can we not live, and join your pleasant party?" asked John. "Why are your laws so severe regarding strangers?"

"We number exactly one hundred—fifty ladies and fifty gentlemen," was the reply. "And, as the island is small, a large number of people would crowd the palace and rendered it uncomfortable. We do not entice strangers here; but neither dare we permit them to escape and tell the world of our pleasant home; for then the ocean would be white with the ships of curious people coming to visit us. So, long ago, the laws were enacted obliging us to destroy whatever strangers chanced upon our retreat. But you are in no immediate danger. As long as your stories last you will live; and while you live you shall enjoy every pleasure our palace affords."

John tried to think how many stories he knew through the virtue of the magic Elixir; but the

startling news he had just heard so confused his
mind that it drove all recollection of romance out
of his head.

"Never mind," whispered Chick.   "All stories
except the true ones have to be made up; so I 'll

make up some.   And don't you worry, John
Dough.   I 've been in worse boxes than this, I can
tell you."

The gingerbread man did n't know exactly what
Chick meant, but the tone of confidence relieved

his embarrassment and inspired him with hope. The ladies and gentlemen set Chick and John in the center of their group and drew their chairs around them and prepared to listen attentively to the child's story.

One might suppose the Incubator Baby's lifetime had been so brief that it knew no stories at all; but Chick was full of imagination and glad of the chance to invent wonderful tales for others to listen to. And the child had resolved to make the stories so long and so interesting that a chance of escape from death might finally be discovered. The flying-machine still rested upon the roof, and if they could manage to regain it there would be no need of their being dumped through the trap-door into the sea.

So Chick began to tell the company a story about an astonishing Silver Pig that once lived in Dagupan (wherever that may be), and was the king of all the pigs of that vast country. His squeal could be heard for seven miles, the child solemnly declared, and the pig's feet were so swift and tireless that he could have run around the world in a single day had there been no oceans to stop him.

The ladies and gentlemen were much interested in the story, and listened very attentively while

The Palace of Romance

Chick related a host of wonderful adventures that befell the Silver Pig. Daylight faded away and the golden lamps were lighted, but still the Incubator Baby kept the story going.

Finally one of the company interrupted the tale to say that it was bedtime and they must all retire, but that Chick should continue the story on the following day.

That was exactly what the Cherub wanted, and presently John and his comrade were escorted to beautiful rooms, and the company of ladies and gentlemen had bidden them a gracious and kindly good-night.

The Silver Pig

"How long is that story of the Silver Pig?" asked John, when they were alone in their room.

"As long as I want to make it," answered Chick, brightly.

"But suppose they get tired of it?" John suggested, timidly.

"Then they'll finish us and the story at the same time," laughed the child. "But we won't wait for that, John Dough. This palace isn't a healthy place for strangers, so I guess the quicker we get away from it the better. When everybody is asleep we'll go to the place where our machine lies, up on the roof, and fly away."

"Very good," agreed John, with a sigh of relief. "I had begun to think we would be killed by these pleasant ladies and gentlemen."

They waited for an hour or two, to be sure all others in the palace were asleep, and then they crept softly from the room and began to search for the staircase. The passages were so alike and so confusing that this was no easy task; but finally, just as they were about to despair, they came upon the stairs and mounted to the upper story of the palace. And now they really became lost in the maze of cross passages that led in every direction; nor could they come to that particular doorway that led to the stairs they had descended from the little flat roof where the flying-machine lay. Often they imagined they had found the right place; but the stairs would lead to some dome or turret that was strange to them, and they would be obliged to retrace their steps.

Morning found the child and the gingerbread man still wandering through the endless passages, and at last they were obliged to abandon the quest and return to their room.

All that following day the fair-haired, blue-eyed Baby continued the strange tale of the Silver Pig, while the ladies and gentlemen of the Palace of Romance seemed to listen with real pleasure. For, long ago, they had told each other all the stories they could themselves remember or imagine; so that it was a rare treat to them to hear of the wonderful adventures of Chick's Silver Pig, and they agreed that the longer the story lasted the better they would be pleased.

The Silver Pig

"I hope you will not die for several days," one lady said to the child, with a sweet smile.

That made Chick laugh.

"Don't you worry about me," was the reply. "If stories will keep me alive I 'll die of old age!"

When bedtime again arrived the tale of the Silver Pig was still unfinished, and once more Chick and the gingerbread man were courteously escorted to their chambers.

They spent the second night in another vain attempt to find the stairs leading to the flat roof, and morning found them as ignorant as ever of the location of their flying-machine.

In spite of the little one's courage, the task of carrying the Silver Pig through so many adventures was a very difficult feat, and the child was weary for lack of sleep. On that third day John fully expected that Chick's invention would become exhausted, and they would both be dropped through the

trap-door into the sea. Chick thought of the sea, too, but the thought gave the child one more idea, and it promptly tumbled the Silver Pig over the side of a ship and landed the adventurous animal upon the bottom of the ocean, where (Chick went on to say) it became acquainted with pretty mermaids and huge green lobsters, and rescued an amarylis from a fierce and disagreeable sea-dragon. This part of the tale soon became really exciting, and when bedtime again arrived the listeners were glad to believe they would hear more of the famous Silver Pig during the following day.

But Chick knew very well that the story had now been stretched out to the very limit, and when they were alone the child took the gingerbread man's hand and said:

"Unless we can find those stairs to-night, John Dough, our jig is up. For by to-morrow evening I'll be at the bottom of the deep blue sea, and the fishes will be having a nice supper of soaked Incubator Baby with gingerbread on the side."

"Please do not mention such a horrible thing," exclaimed John, with a shiver. "The stairs are surely in existence, for once we came down them; so let us make one more careful search for them."

This they did, walking for hours up and down the passages, pulling aside every drapery they came to, but never finding the slender staircase that led to the flat roof.

Even when it grew daylight they did not abandon the quest; for they could see their way much better than when feeling along dim passages by the uncertain light of the moon; and, as the danger grew every moment, they redoubled their eagerness in the quest.

All at once they heard footsteps approaching; and, as they were standing in the middle of a long passage, they pressed back against the marble wall to escape discovery. At once the wall gave way, and John tumbled backward into another passage, with the Cherub sprawling on top of him. For they had backed against a drapery painted to represent a wall of the outer passage, and now found themselves in a place they had not before explored.

Hastily regaining their feet, the fugitives ran down the passage, and at the end came suddenly upon another heavy drapery, which, when thrust aside, was found to conceal the identical flight of steps they had sought for so long and unsuccessfully.

Uttering cries of joy, Chick and John quickly

mounted the stairs and found themselves upon the flat roof.

The flying bird lay as they had left it, and they were about to crawl inside when the sound of footsteps mounting the stairs was heard.

"Quick!" shouted the child. "Jump in, John Dough!"

"Is it safe?" asked John, who remembered how they had bumped upon the roof.

"Well, it's either air or water for us, my friend, and I prefer the air," laughed Chick, whose cheeks were red with exitement.

John hesitated no longer and was soon inside the bird's body. Chick scrambled after and at once pressed the electric button, while John threw over the silver lever.

The big wings began to flop just as a number of men came upon the roof, uttering loud cries at the evident attempt of their prisoners to escape. But the strong pinions of the bird swept them flat, like so many ten-pins, and before they could get upon their feet again the flying-machine was high in the air and well out of their reach.

THE ESCAPE

Pittypat and the Mifkets

NOTICE PRIVATE!

"This invention works better than I thought it would, after getting that bump," John remarked, as they flew onward over the vast expanse of rolling waves.

"It's a bit wobbly, though," said Chick. "Don't you notice it flops a little sideways?"

"Yes," answered John, "and it seems to me the bird does not move so swiftly as it did at first."

"Guess the 'lectricity's giving out," returned Chick, calmly. "If it does, what'll happen?"

"We'll be drowned, I suppose," said John. "I don't understand electricity, for the wisdom I derive from the magic Elixir dates far back beyond the discovery of electric fluid."

"Your wisdom's bald-headed, I'm afraid," observed the child, smiling at the solemn countenance of the gingerbread man. "But, say! Isn't

166

that another island over there?" Chick continued, after a look through one of the little windows.

"It appears to be an island," replied John, also gazing through the window.

Even as he spoke the bird gave a lurch and swooped downward toward the sea, tipping at such an angle that Chick and the gingerbread man were both tumbled off their seats. John's glass eyes had a look of fear in them, but Chick laughed as merrily as if there was no danger at all, and began pushing the electric buttons with great vigor, one after another.

The result was that the flying-machine paused, righted itself, plunged higher into the air, circled around a few times, and then sailed rapidly toward the west. Chick scrambled back to the seat and threw over the steering wheel in order to make the machine head directly toward the island they had seen.

"If we can keep her going till we get to that island, I don't care what happens afterward," said the child. "But if we're dumped in the sea I'm afraid we can't swim far."

"I can't swim at all," John returned; "for in three strokes my gingerbread would become soaked through and fall to pieces. And the water would

167

dilute the Elixir that I am mixed with and destroy all its magic powers. By the way, what's the thing doing now?"

"It's getting more wobbly. But never mind. It's lots of fun, is n't it, John Dough?"

"Not exactly fun," said John, seriously; "but I will admit this voyage is rather exciting."

Just then something snapped, and they heard a rapid whir of machinery inside the bird, a squeak that sounded like a wail of despair, and then a dull crash.   The big machine trembled, ceased flopping its wings, and remained poised in the air like an immense kite.

"It's all up," said Chick.   "The thing's busted."

"What's going to happen?" asked John, anxiously.

"Wait and see," returned Chick, with a laugh.

"It's cruel to laugh when we are in such grave danger!" said John, reproachfully.

"Shucks!" cried the child.   "It might be my last laugh, and I'd be foolish to miss it."

The bird was still floating, for its broad wings were rigidly spread out to their fullest extent; but every moment the machine sailed nearer to the sea, and although it was surely nearing the island, neither John nor Chick could decide whether it would finally succeed in reaching the shore or fall into the water.

Even the careless Cherub paused with bated breath to watch the final catastrophe, and John, resigned to whatever fate might befall him, nevertheless passed the most anxious moments of his brief lifetime.

The bird sailed down, rested upon the water a few feet from the shore, and floated upon the surface.

169

Pittypat and the Mifkets

Chick and John dared not open the door for fear of letting in the ocean and so being drowned. Neither could they now see where they were, for the green water pressed close against the little windows. So they sat silently within the machine until there came a sudden jar and the bird rolled over upon one side and lay still.

"We're saved!" cried the Cherub. For now one of the windows was raised above the water and enabled them to see that the bird had drifted to the shore of the island and was fast upon the beach.

Chick unfastened the door and crawled out; and then the child assisted John to leap from the machine to the shore without even wetting his feet. And it was indeed fortunate they acted so promptly, as no sooner were they safely upon the island than a big wave dashed up, caught the broken flying-machine in its grasp, and rolled it out to sea again, where it quickly sank to the bottom and disappeared from their view forever.

"That's all right," said the child. "I wouldn't care to ride in the thing again, anyhow. Would you, John Dough?"

"No," answered the gingerbread man. "But what a shame it was to accuse Imar of being a successful inventor! If the Kinglet of Phreex

CHICK ASSISTS JOHN TO LAND

could have watched our flight he would know that Imar has n't solved the flying-machine problem yet."

"Still, it carried us away from two bad places," said Chick, "and that's all we wanted of it. Come on, John Dough; let's go and explore our island."

It did not take our adventurers long to discover they were in a really remarkable place. Near the shore was a strip of land that at first sight seemed thickly covered with grass; but when Chick examined it closely it was found to be a mass of tiny trees set close together, and each tree was full of small and tender green leaves. And, as the trees were only an inch or two high, they really looked like grass from a distance and proved to be soft and pleasant to walk upon.

But behind this green sward towered a forest so strange and magnificent that both Chick and John Dough held their breaths in amazed awe as they gazed upon it. For they beheld a confused group of the most gorgeous plants imaginable, most of them having broad leaves as big as the sails of a ship and of exceedingly vivid colorings. There were violet and carmine leaves side by side with brilliant yellows and pinks, blues and ambers, and among them great bunches of pure white leaves that

in fairness rivaled those of a lily. Some of the huge
forest plants were low and broad—no taller than
an ordinary house—but many of them shot up
into the sky like spires and church steeples. And
another strange thing was the fact that they were all
filled with clusters of flowers of many beautiful
shapes and designs. And the flowers were of
various tints of greens—running from a delicate
pea-green through all the different shades to bright
emerald, and then to deep bottle-greens. Yet the
flowers were the only green colors in all the vast
forest of brilliant plants—which glowed so magnifi-
cently under the rays of the sun that the eyes of
our friends were fairly dazzled as they gazed.

"My!" gasped Chick. "Isn't it splendiferous,
John Dough?"

"It is, indeed very gorgeous and beautiful,"
answered the gingerbread man. "But has it occurred to you, little friend, that there may be nothing for you to eat in all this wilderness of color."

"Eat?" exclaimed Chick. "Why, John Dough,
I'm hungry this very minute! I haven't had a bite
to eat since I left the Palace of Romance, and
now you mention it, I'm half starved. But perhaps there isn't a smitch of oatmeal or cream on
all this island!"

"Could n't you eat anything else?" asked John.

"Oh, I could, I suppose. But other food might make me ill, you know. Incubator Babies have to be very careful of their diet."

"But if you don't eat you will die," said John; "so it will be best for you to dine upon whatever you may find."

"There may be fruits in the forest," said Chick, thoughtfully; "but it's such a queer forest that quite likely the fruits are poisonous."

"Still, you'd better try them," persisted the gingerbread man. "If you don't you'll die; and if you are poisoned you'll die. But there is a chance of your finding healthful fruits instead of poisonous ones. I regret that in all my store of wisdom, derived from the Arabian Elixir, there is no knowledge of such a forest or the fruits these gay plants may bear."

"Well, you wait here till I come back," said Chick, more cheerfully. "I'll explore and see what I can find. There's no need to worry until the time comes, anyhow."

With that the little one waved a chubby hand toward John Dough, and then ran into the forest and disappeared beneath the great purple and orange colored leaves.

Pittypat and the Mifkets

And now it occurred to the gingerbread man to make an examination of himself and see what an extent of damage he had suffered since he had come, hot and fresh, from Monsieur Jules' bakery.

His lovely shirt-front was cracked in several places and speckled with tiny black spots where the powder of the rocket had burned it. His left shoulder was also blackened with burned powder, and he had lost one of the lozenge buttons from his red vest. Also, one of his heels was slightly crumbled, and there were three marks in his body where the diamonds had been pressed into him, beside the lance-thrust of the Blunderer.

These damages were not at all

serious, however, and he was beginning to con-
gratulate himself upon his escape, when he discovered a curious sensation in his nose. Raising
his hand, he found that the extreme end of his
nose had been chipped off in some way during
his escape from the Palace of Romance, and this
rather marred his personal appearance. The
discovery made him sigh regretfully; and when he
looked around, in the newly arrived sunlight, it
seemed that his vision had become in some way
twisted and unnatural. He could not understand
this at first, and rose to his feet rather dazed and
unhappy. Then an idea occurred to him, and he
felt of his glass eyes and found that one — the left
eye — had become loose in its socket and turned
inward, making him cross-eyed. He remedied this
by turning it with his fingers until it looked
straight ahead again, and matched the other eye;
but often thereafter that left eye would get
twisted and bother him until he turned it straight
again.

While he awaited Chick's return, John strolled
to the edge of the forest and sat down upon a big
yellow mushroom that was strong enough to bear
his weight. It seemed to be a peaceful island, and
the gingerbread man was well pleased with his

surroundings, having at that time no idea of all the desperate adventures that were to befall him before he saw the last of those brilliant shores.

From his feet the beach sloped gently to meet the waves of the blue ocean, and on the sands were many shells of curious shapes and colors. The breath of the wind was full of the fragrance of the flowers, and in the forest plants many birds sang sweet songs.

As he watched the waves, the birds, and the flowers, John heard a slight rustling sound, and turning his glass eyes downward saw at his feet a small animal which sat upon its haunches and regarded him with big and earnest eyes.

"Who are you?" asked the gingerbread man; "and what is your name?"

"My name is Pittypat, and I'm a rabbit," answered the animal. "But tell me, please, who *you* are, and what may be your name; for I have never seen your like before."

"I am a gingerbread man, and my name is John Dough," he replied, readily. And then, more anxiously, he asked: "Do you eat gingerbread, friend Pittypat?"

"No, indeed," was the reply. "I prefer clover and sweet roots. But please answer another question. How is that you understand my language, and can talk to me?"

"I cannot tell you that, I'm sure," said John, "unless it's the effect of the Elixir. That seems to be responsible for almost everything, you know."

Pittypat and the Mifkets

The rabbit did not know, of course, and looked at its new acquaintance in a puzzled sort of way.

"Are there any more like you on this island?" inquired John Dough

"Oh, yes; there are lots of us!" exclaimed the rabbit. "But not so many of us as there are Mifkets."

"And what is a Mifket?" asked John.

"A sort of creature that is neither an animal nor a man," answered Pittypat. "And the Mifkets rule this island because they are bigger and fiercer than we rabbits are. Also I know many squirrels and birds and mice, and the Fairy King of the beavers — for I am well acquainted here. But I do not like the Mifkets, and scamper away when they come near. There is a bouncing brown bear, also, who lives on a hill yonder, and once he claimed to be king of all the animals. But the Mifkets found out that our bear is not nearly so dreadful as he seems; so they refused to obey him, and now have a king of their own. For my part, however, I like the brown bear best of all our inhabitants, for he has a jolly nature and never hurts any one."

"But are there no men — no people like *me* upon this island?" asked John.

"No one like you, most surely," answered Pittypat, staring at the gingerbread man with its big eyes. "But as for human creatures, there are three who dwell with the Mifkets, near the other side of the forest."

"Dear me!" sighed John; "I'm sorry to hear that. Who are the humans?"

"Well, one is the Princess, and the Princess is very beautiful and lovely," answered Pittypat. "She isn't much bigger than the child I saw here with you a few minutes ago; but our little Princess is beloved by every creature on the island — except, perhaps, the Mifkets, who love only themselves."

"Does the Princess live in a palace?" asked John.

"Oh, yes; a beautiful palace made by bending downward the big leaves of the roi-tree and fastening the ends to the ground. One of the leaves is left loose, for a doorway, and in the room thus formed the Princess lives in great state and loneliness, and sleeps upon a bed of fragrant mosses."

"Does she like gingerbread?" inquired John, after a thoughtful pause.

"I don't believe she knows what gingerbread is," the rabbit replied. "But you may be sure the Princess will not harm you, however fond she might be of gingerbread."

THE HOME OF THE PRINCESS 181

Pittypat and the Mifkets

"I'm glad to hear that," said John. "But your Princess is the only one of the three human creatures you mentioned. Who are the others?"

"Her father and mother," said the rabbit. "The three landed here in a small boat some years ago. They were shipwrecked, I suppose, and the boat is still lying upon the north shore. But the terrible Mifkets captured the father and mother of the Princess and made them slaves, to wait upon them and obey their wishes; and as the little girl was delicate and not very strong, they let her live by herself in the palace of the roi-tree, and mocked her by calling her a Princess. If she grows up to be strong I think they will make her a slave, too; but she is so frail and weak that none of us rabbits believe she will live very long."

"This is all very interesting," said John. "I'd really like to meet these humans."

"Then come with me and I will guide your steps to where they are," promised the rabbit.

"I must wait until Chick comes back," said the gingerbread man, looking toward the plant forest.

"Is Chick the child I saw going into the forest?" asked the rabbit.

"Yes," replied John. "It's an Incubator Baby

and very jolly and kind. Chick ought to be back in a few minutes."

"I'm rather nervous when children are around," declared the rabbit, hesitating. "Are you sure Chick is kind?"

"Very," said John, with conviction; "so don't you worry, friend Rabbit."

At that moment the Cherub came running up with both hands full of fruits, which were indeed odd in shape, but delicious in odor and enticing in appearance.

"I won't starve, John Dough!" was the merry greeting. "The forest is full of fruit plants, and I've eaten some already, and haven't been poisoned. But where did you find this pretty rabbit? And how tame it seems to be!"

"It's a friend of mine named Pittypat, and I've discovered I can speak its language," replied John. "Also there's a Princess living near by, and Pittypat has promised to guide us to her royal palace."

"All right!" exclaimed Chick, busily eating of the fruit. "Let's go now."

John turned to the little animal beside him and said, in the rabbit language: "We are ready to start, my friend."

Pittypat and the Mifkets

"You'll have to meet the Mifkets, you know," said Pittypat, rather fearfully.

"Never mind; we're not afraid," answered John, boldly; and Chick, who as yet had heard nothing of the Mifkets, continued to munch the fruit with perfect composure.

So the rabbit whisked around, lifted its big ears a moment, sniffed the air, and then sprang away with long and graceful leaps along a tiny path that led through the magnificent forest.

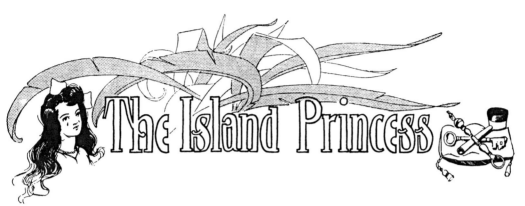

The Island Princess

John settled the baker's hat (which was showing distinct signs of having been frequently crumpled) upon his gingerbread head, picked up the remains of his candy cane, and followed the guidance of the white rabbit. Chick came after, tripping lightly along the path. Before they had gone very far beneath the bright-hued, mammoth foliage Pittypat gave a sudden whisk and disappeared from sight, having popped into a hole. John Dough, of course, stopped and gazed around with his glass eyes to see what had become of his new friend, and at the same moment a queer creature dropped from an overhead leaf and stood in the path of the gingerbread man. Another followed, and still another, and the three strange beings looked at John curiously, as if as much surprised at the meeting as he could be. Chick pressed close to the side of the gingerbread man and stared with big eyes at the new arrivals.

Perhaps nowhere else in all the world could be

185

found such unusual creatures as these Mifkets. Their heads had the appearance of cocoanuts, and were covered with coarse hair clipped close, and turning upward until it ended in a sharp peak at the very top. Their faces were like putty, with small, beady eyes that glittered brightly, flat noses, and wide, grinning mouths. The Mifkets bodies

were shaped like pears, and their legs were short and their arms long. For clothing they wore gay leaves of the forest plants, twisted and woven together in quite a clever way; and taken all together, they were as unlike any creatures that inhabit our part of the world as can well be imagined.

"Ah, these must be the beings called Mifkets," remarked John Dough, speaking aloud in a language he had never used before, but that seemed well fitted to such creatures.

"That's easy enough to guess," retorted one of the group, coming nearer to the gingerbread man and impudently thrusting forward its putty-like face, which it wrinkled and distorted in a disturbing manner. "It's easy enough to tell we're Mifkets; but what in the name of Jucklethub are you? And what strange child of the human's is this with you?"

"I'm a gingerbread man," answered John, with dignity; "and this is my friend Chick."

"We know what a man is; and we know what a child is; but what's gingerbread?" demanded another of the Mifkets.

"*I'm* gingerbread," said John.

187

"We'll take your word for it," growled the third creature. And then it added: "What are you doing here?"

"Standing still, just now," said John, gravely.

To his surprise all three began laughing at this reply, and they seemed so greatly amused that one hit another a merry cuff upon the ear, which he in turn passed on to the third. But the third—the growling one—turned suddenly upon John Dough and gave him such a sounding cuff upon the side of his head that the blow dazed him for a moment. At this Chick doubled two fat fists and ran at the queer Mifkets so fiercely that they were greatly astonished at the angry buffets they received, and fell back a few steps from the path. Immediately John Dough recovered his wits and aimed a strong blow with the candy cane at the wild people of the forest. Much to his astonishment it sent all three of them tumbling to the ground—one overturning the others. For so great was the energy and strength lent to his gingerbread arm by the magic Elixir that the Mifkets could not stand before it.

Chick laughed merrily at the howls of their enemies, who quickly scrambled to their feet and leaped into the leaves of the giant plants, where they were hidden from sight. But the sound of their rapid retreat could be heard until it died away in the distance.

Then the rabbit stuck its nose from the hole in which it had hidden and said:

"Bravely done, little one. Bravely done, John Dough. Yet I warn you to beware these wicked Mifkets, who will now consider you both their enemies."

"I don't care," said Chick; "and I'm not afraid," added John, who was quite pleased to find himself so powerful.

"Well, let us continue our journey," suggested Pittypat; "for I want you to meet our sweet Princess. But I advise you, whenever you meet with more of those Mifkets, to try to be friendly with them. There are hundreds of them, you know, and only two of you."

"That sounds like good advice," acknowledged John.

Again they started along the path, and presently it led them out of the forest to another part of the shore of the island, where a rocky headland curved into the sea in the shape of a new moon, forming a pretty bay, on which floated a small boat at anchor. On the inner edge of this headland and facing the bay stood a tall plant, whose broad colored leaves were bent downward to form a dome-shaped room, one leaf being turned up to make an opening that served as a door.

"You must whistle at the door, and the Princess

will appear," said Pittypat. "I cannot talk with her as I do with you, Mr. Dough; so I 'll leave you now, and run home to tell my folks of the new friends I have found." With these parting words away darted the rabbit, and John and Chick shyly approached the novel palace of the Princess.

"Can you whistle, Chick?" asked the gingerbread man; and the Baby, in reply, made so shrill a sound through the puckered pink lips that John gave a start of surprise.

Almost immediately a girl appeared in the door-way of the plant-palace, and both John and Chick bowed low and then stood motionless to stare at the beautiful face that confronted them. For this mock Princess of the Mifkets was quite the loveliest and sweetest maiden that any one has ever looked upon; and so round and innocent were her clear eyes and so gentle and winning her smile, that to see her but once was to love her dearly. John did not marvel that the wild crea-tures of the forest had set this girl apart as too hal-lowed to become either their slave or companion; and he instantly accepted this shipwrecked waif as a real Princess, and from that moment worshipped loyally at her shrine.

Chick, standing solidly with brown feet spread wide apart, chubby fists clutching the last of the forest fruits, and tangled locks flowing carelessly around the laughing face, was a strong contrast to the little lady who advanced from the door with dainty steps to welcome the strangers. The Princess wore a gown of woven leaves plucked from the island plants, but so slight and graceful was her form that any sort of dress would be sure to seem fit and becoming if the maid wore it.

"Hello!" said Chick. "We've come to see you."

"I'm glad of that," answered the girl, in a soft voice, as she came close and kissed the Cherub's rosy mouth. "It has been dreadfully lonesome in this place without any one to play with or to keep me company. But may I inquire who you are?"

"This is John Dough," answered the Cherub, briefly; "and I'm Chick."

"I'm pleased to make your acquaintance," said the girl. "They call me the Princess; but that is in mockery, I am sure."

"But are you not treated as a Princess?" asked John.

"Yes; and that is why I am so lonely," the girl replied, sadly. "The naughty Mifkets have made my poor father and mother their slaves, and mock me by shutting me in this tree-house and calling it a palace and me a Princess. But really I am as much a slave as either of my dear parents."

"Can't you go out if you want to?" asked Chick.

"Oh, yes; but the island is small, and there is no one to play with except Pittypat, who is a white rabbit, and Para Bruin, who is a bouncing brown bear."

"What strange companions!" said John. "I've met Pittypat, and like the white rabbit very much; but a bouncing brown bear must be a dreadful creature."

"Not at all, I assure you," returned the girl, earnestly. "Just wait until you meet him, and you'll see that he couldn't hurt any one if he would, and wouldn't if he could."

"That's all right," said Chick.

"But do the Mifkets illtreat you in any way?" asked John.

"Oh, no; until now they have done me no real injury whatever," the Princess answered, "but their tempers are so hateful that I am in constant fear of them. You must meet the Mifkets, of course, since you cannot leave this island; and you must obey them as we all do. But perhaps Mr. Dough, being made of gingerbread, will be treated with more respect than human beings are."

"Or with less," said John, with a shudder. "Nevertheless, we will meet the Mifkets boldly, and I am not going to make myself unhappy by being afraid of them."

"Nor I," said Chick. "They're only beasts."

"Then, if you will please follow me, I will lead you to the king's village," said the girl; "and there you may see my father and mother."

"Very well," agreed John. "But I must tell you that we have already encountered three of these creatures, and defeated them easily."

"I pounded 'em like sixty," added the Cherub, with a nod and a laugh.

The Princess led them by a path deep into the forest, passing underneath the broad leaves of the plants, which were so thick that they almost shut out the daylight and made the way gloomy and fearsome. But before long a big clearing was reached, in the center of which was a rocky mound with a broad, flat stone at the very top. All around were houses made by bending down the

THE KING OF THE MIFKETS

huge leaves of the plants and fastening them to the
ground with wooden pegs, thus forming circular
rooms. None of these houses seemed quite so
handsome as the palace of the Princess; but they
were big and of many colors, and when our
friends stepped into the clearing a swarm of the
Mifket people crowded out of the doorways to
surround the strangers and gaze upon them
curiously.

Upon the flat stone in the center of the clearing reclined an aged Mifket, who was lazily sunning
himself, and who seemed to pay no attention to the
chattering of his fellows. Yet it was toward this
stone that the Princess, after a half-frightened look
at its occupant, led her new friends; and all the
Mifkets, big and little, followed them and formed a
circle around them and the aged one.

"This is the King," whispered the girl. "Be
careful not to anger him."

Then she knelt humbly before the flat stone that
served as a throne, and John Dough knelt beside
her. But Chick stood upright and laughed at the
sight of the lazy Mifket King reclining before them.

The short, coarse hair that covered the head of
the King was white, proving him to be very old;
and his raiment was woven of pure white leaves,

distinguishing him from all the others of his band. But he was not especially dignified in appearance.

Hearing the murmur around him the King slowly rolled his fat body over and sat up, rubbing his eyes to clear them of the cobwebs of sleep. Then he looked upon John and Chick and gave a grunt. Immediately a little man rushed out of a dwelling just back of the throne and hurried to the King with a gourd filled with water. This the aged Mifket drank greedily, and while he was thus occupied the Princess grasped the hand of the little man and pressed it affectionately.

"This is my father," she whispered to John Dough and Chick.

The little man seemed fussy and nervous, but perhaps this was caused by the fear in which he constantly lived. There was little hair upon his head, but he wore chin whiskers that were bright red in color and luxuriant in growth, and harmonized nicely with his light blue eyes. He wore

a faded and ragged suit of blue clothes, to which
he had doubtless clung ever since the days when
he had been shipwrecked and cast upon this island.

John Dough was about to express in polite
words his pleasure in meeting the father of the
Princess, when the King, having finished drinking,
suddenly flung the gourd at the little man's head.
He ducked to escape it and the gourd struck the
forehead of a big Mifket just behind and made a
sound like the crack of a whip. At once the big
Mifket — who was remarkable for having black hair
upon his head instead of the dingy brown that
was common to all the Mifkets — uttered a roar of
rage and aimed a blow at the bald head of the
luckless slave. But the little man ducked this
blow also, and then scampered away to the
royal dwelling as fast as his thin legs could carry
him.

"Let him go," said the King, speaking sleepily in
the Mifket language. Then he turned to the black
one and asked: "Who are these creatures, Ooboo?
and how came they here?"

"I don't know," answered Black Ooboo, sulkily;
"the girl brought them."

"Perhaps I can explain," said John Dough,
speaking in their language. "My friend Chick and

THE MIFKETS HOWLED WITH DELIGHT

The Island Princess

I arrived here but a short time ago in a flying-machine, which unfortunately broke down and prevented us from getting away again."

The Mifkets looked at the gingerbread man in astonishment. Not because they had any idea what a flying-machine might be, but to hear their own language spoken by so queer a personage, filled them with amazement.

"Are you one of those miserable creatures called humans?" asked the King, blinking his eyes at the gingerbread man.

"I cannot, in truth, claim to be precisely human," replied John, "but it is certain that I possess a degree of human wisdom. It comes from the Elixir, you know."

"What are you made of?" demanded the King, who was certainly puzzled by John's words.

Now, the gingerbread man realized that if he told the Mifkets he was good to eat he would soon be destroyed; so he answered:

"I am made of a kind of material known only to civilized men. In fact, I am very different from all the rest of the world."

The King didn't understand, and when he didn't understand it made him very tired.

"Oh, well," said he, lying back in the sun, "just

make yourself at home here, and see that you don't bother me by getting in my way."

That might have ended the interview had not Black Ooboo, scowling and angry, stepped forward and said:

"If the stranger is to live with us he must fight for the right to live in peace. It is our custom, your Majesty."

"So it is," returned the King, waking up again. "The stranger must fight."

At this decision all the Mifkets howled with delight, and Chick and the Princess began to be uneasy about their friend. But John said, calmly:

"I have never fought with any one, your Majesty; but I'll do the best I can. With whom must I fight?"

"Why, with Black Ooboo, I suppose," said the King; "and if you can manage to give him a sound thrashing I'll be your friend for life."

Ooboo scowled first at the King and then at John, and all the other Mifkets scowled with him, for the black one was seemingly a great favorite among them.

"Whatever material you may be made of, bold stranger," he said, "I promise to crush you into bits and trample you into the dust."

Then the crowd having pressed backward, the black Mifket sprang upon the gingerbread man, with long, hairy arms outstretched as if to clutch him. But John was quicker than his foe. He grasped Ooboo about the waist, lifted him high in

202

the air — big and heavy though he was — and flung him far over the throne whereon the King squatted. The black one crashed into the leaves of a forest plant and then tumbled to the ground, where he lay still for a moment to recover from his surprise and the shock of defeat.

The rabble of Mifkets didn't applaud the fall of their champion, but they looked upon the gingerbread man with wonder. And the King was so pleased that he laughed aloud.

"Well done, stranger," said he. "Ooboo needed to be taken down a peg, and you did it very neatly. Now get away, all of you, and leave me to sleep." He proceeded to curl himself up once more upon the flat stone, and the Mifkets obeyed his command and stole away to their dwellings. John advanced to where Chick and the Princess stood, and the Cherub patted him on the hand and said:

"I'd no idea you could do it, John. Wasn't it lovely, Princess, to see him toss that black beast like a football?"

"I'm glad your friend won the fight," answered the girl; "but Black Ooboo is a dangerous enemy, and even the King is afraid of him. Now come with me, please. I want you to meet my dear mother, who is unfortunately degraded to the position of the King's cook."

They entered with the Princess into the royal dwelling, where a woman quickly seized the girl in a warm embrace and kissed her tenderly. When Chick managed to get a full view of the woman she was seen to be nearly as round as an apple in form, with an apple's rosy cheeks, and with cute corkscrew curls of an iron-gray color running from her ears down to her neck. When her daughter entered she had been busily engaged cooking a vegetable stew for the King's dinner, nor dared she pause long in her work for fear of the King's anger.

Chick was dreadfully sorry for these poor shipwrecked people, thus compelled to be slaves to the fierce Mifkets, and hoped they might find some way

to escape. The little man with the red whiskers presently crept in and joined them, and they had a long talk together and tried to think of a plan to leave the island, but without success.

The Island Princess

Yet John encouraged them to believe a way would soon be found, and they all had great confidence in his ability to save the entire party; for he had proved himself both wise and powerful.

While they were still talking the King rolled his fat body into the dwelling and demanded his dinner, at the same time ordering the Princess to get back to her own palace and to stay there. But he favored John Dough by sending several of the Mifkets to build a dwelling for the gingerbread man and the Incubator Baby just beside that of the little Princess, which pleased them all very much.

Para Bruin, the Rubber Bear

Next morning the little Princess came to the door of the new dwelling built for Chick and John Dough, and said to them:

"Let us take a walk, and I will show you how beautiful our island is in those parts where there are no Mifkets to worry us."

So together the three walked along the shore until they drew near to a high point of rock, the summit of which was reached by a winding path. When they had climbed up the steep the Princess had to stop to rest, for she was not strong and seemed to tire easily. And now, while they sat upon some rocks, a big brown bear came out of a cave and stood before them.

"Don't be afraid," whispered the Princess. "He won't hurt us. It's Para Bruin."

The bear was fat and of monstrous size, and its color was a rich brown. It had no hair at all upon its body, as most bears have, but was smooth and shiny. He gave a yawn as he looked at the

206

Para Bruin, the Rubber Bear

new-comers, and John shuddered at the rows of long, white teeth that showed so plainly. Also he noticed the fierce claws upon the bear's toes, and decided that in spite of the rabbit's and the Princess' assurances he was in dangerous company. Indeed, although Chick laughed at the bear, the gingerbread man grew quite nervous as the big beast advanced and sniffed at him curiously — almost as if it realized John was made of gingerbread and that gingerbread is good to eat.  Then it held out a fat paw, as if desiring to shake hands; and, not wishing to appear rude, John placed his own hand in the bear's paw, which seemed even more soft and flabby than his own. The next moment the animal threw its great arms around the gingerbread man and hugged him close to its body.

Para Bruin, the Rubber Bear

John gave a cry of fear, although it was hard to tell which was more soft and yielding— the bear's fat body or the form of the gingerbread man.

"Stop that!" he shouted, speaking in the bear language. "Let me go, instantly! What do you mean by such actions?"

The bear, hearing this speech, at once released John, who began to feel of himself to see if he had been damaged by the hug.

"Why didn't you say you were a friend, and could speak my language?" asked the bear, in a tone of reproach.

"You knew well enough I was a friend, since I came with the Princess," retorted John, angrily. "I suppose you would like to eat me, just because I am gingerbread!"

"I thought you smelled like gingerbread," remarked the bear. "But don't worry about my eating you. I don't eat."

"No?" said John, surprised. "Why not?"

"Well, the principal reason is that I'm made of rubber," said the bear.

"Rubber!" exclaimed John.

"Yes, rubber. Not gutta-percha, you understand, nor any cheap composition; but pure Para

208

"STOP THAT!" JOHN SHOUTED

209

rubber of the best quality. I'm practically in-destructible."

"Well, I declare!" said John, who was really astonished. "Are your teeth rubber, also?"

"To be sure," acknowledged the bear, seeming to be somewhat ashamed of the fact; "but they appear very terrible to look at, do they not? No one would suspect they would bend if I tried to bite with them."

"To me they were terrible in appearance," said John, at which the bear seemed much gratified.

"I don't mind confiding to you, who are a friend and speak my language," he resumed, "that I am as harmless as I am indestructible. But I pride myself upon my awful appearance, which should strike terror into the hearts of all beholders. At one time every creature in this island feared me, and acknowledged me their king; but those horrid Mifkets discovered I was rubber, and have defied me ever since."

"How came you to be alive?" asked John. "Was it the Great Elixir?"

"I've never heard of the Great Elixir," replied the bear, "and I've no idea how I came to be alive. My earliest recollection is that I was living in much the same way that I am now. Do you remember when you were not living?"

Para Bruin, the Rubber Bear

"No," said John.

This conversation, which she could not at all understand, surprised the Princess very much. But she was glad to see that the rubber bear and the gingerbread man had become friends, and so she took Chick's hand and led the smiling Cherub up to where they stood.

"This is my new friend, whose name is Chick," she said to the bear, for the girl was accustomed to talking to Para Bruin just as she would to a person; "and you must be as good and kind to Chick as you have been to me, my dear Para, or I shall not love you any more."

The bear gave the Princess a generous hug, and then he hugged Chick; but the words the girl had spoken seemed to puzzle him, for he turned to John and said:

"Why do you suppose so many different languages were ever invented? The Mifkets speak one language, and you and I speak another, and the Princess and Chick speak still another! And it is all very absurd, for the only language I can understand is my own."

"I can speak with and understand the Princess and the Mifkets as well as I can speak with you," declared John.

Para Bruin, the Rubber Bear

The bear looked at him admiringly.

"If that is so, then tell me what the Princess said to me just now," he requested.

So John translated the girl's words into the bear language, and when Para Bruin heard them he laughed with delight.

"Tell the Princess that I'll be as good to her friend Chick as possible," said he, and John at once translated it so that the Princess understood.

"That's nice," said she. "I knew Para would be friends with Chick. And now ask the bear to bounce for us. He does it often, and it is a very interesting sight."

So John requested the bear to bounce, which he at once agreed to do, seeming to feel considerable pride in the accomplishment.

From the point upon which they stood, the hill descended in a steep incline toward the forest, and at the bottom of the hill was a big flat rock. Curling himself into a ball, the great bear rolled his body down the hill, speeding faster every moment, until he struck the flat rock at the bottom. Then he bounded high into the air (in the same way that a rubber ball does when thrown down upon a hard pavement), and made a graceful backward curve until he reached the top

Para Bruin, the Rubber Bear

of the hill again, where he bounced up and down a few times, and then stood upright and bowed before the gingerbread man and the gleeful Cherub —who was rapturously delighted by the performance.

"Great act, is n't it?" asked Para Bruin, grinning with pride. "No ordinary bear could do that, I assure you. And it proves the purity and high grade of my rubber."

"It does, indeed!" declared John. "I am greatly pleased to have met so remarkable and talented a bear."

Para Bruin, the Rubber Bear

"You must visit me often," said the bear, making a dignified bow. "It is a great treat to hear my own language spoken, for I am the only bear upon the island. I haven't any visiting cards, but my name is Para Bruin, and you are always welcome at my cave."

"I am called John Dough," said the gingerbread man. "I cannot claim to be indestructible, but while I last I shall be proud of your friendship, and will bring the children to visit you often."

"Try to teach them my language," suggested Para Bruin; "for I love children and have often wished I might talk with them. As for the little Princess, all the island people love her dearly—except, of course, the Mifkets—and we all worry, more or less, over her health. She's weak and delicate, you know; and her life here is made so unhappy by the separation from her parents that I'm afraid she won't be with us very long."

He wiped a tear from his eye with a puffy paw and glanced affectionately at the girl.

"What's the matter with her?" asked John, anxiously.

"No strength and vitality," answered the bear. "She's failing every day, and there isn't a drug-store or a doctor on the island. But don't tell her, whatever you do. Perhaps she does n't realize it, and the knowledge would only make her more unhappy."

Then the bear, wno seemed remarkably tender-hearted, trotted with bouncing footsteps into his cave, so that the little Princess for whom he grieved might not see the tears that stood in his rubber eyes.

After that John and Chick and the Princess started to return to their dwellings by means of a short cut through the forest, known to the girl. John was feeling very contented in the companion-ship of the two children, and reflected that in spite of the Mifkets his life on this beautiful island bade fair to be pleasant and agreeable. But his content

was suddenly inter-rupted by the Cherub, who gave a loud cry and pointed excitedly into the forest.

The gingerbread man had cast but one look when he began to tremble violently. For there

215

before him—only a few paces away—stood his bitter and relentless enemy, Ali Dubh the Arab!

"At last," said Ali Dubh, smiling most unpleasantly, "I have again found you."

John was too agitated to reply; but Chick asked, boldly:

"How on earth did you ever get to this island?"

"By means of the witch," the Arab replied. "I purchased from her two transport powders. One transported me to the Isle of Phreex, and when you then escaped me the other powder transported me here. But I cannot allow the gingerbread man to escape me again, because I have no more powders, nor any way to reach the witch who makes them. So, my dear John Dough, please accept your fate, and permit me to eat you at once."

"That I cannot do," said John, firmly; "for if I am eaten, that is the end of me."

"How selfish!" exclaimed the Arab. "Who are you, to be considered before Ali Dubh, son of a mighty Shiek, and chief of an ancient Tribe of the Desert? Remember, sir, that when I have eaten you I shall gain for myself the priceless powers of that Great Elixir contained in your gingerbread, and

ALI DUBH ATTACKS JOHN

will thus become the most powerful and most intelligent man in the world, besides living forever! Dare you, sir, allow your selfish motives to interfere with so grand a result?"

"I dare," replied John.

"But you have nothing to say about it," continued the Arab. "You are not your own master. You belong to me, for I purchased you from Jules Grogrande, the baker, who made you, and I am therefore entitled to eat you whenever I please."

"Nevertheless," answered John, "I will not be eaten if I can help it."

"Ah! but that is unjust!" protested the Arab.

"If to be unjust is to be eaten," said John, "you need not look to me for justice. I may be wrong in this decision, but it is better to be wrong than to be nothing."

"Then," remarked Ali Dubh, sadly, "you force me to eat you without your consent, which it will grieve me to do."

With this he drew his terrible knife and sprang upon John Dough with great ferocity. But in the recent encounter with Black Ooboo the gingerbread man had learned how powerful the Elixir made him; so he did not run this time from the Arab, but avoided the thrust of the knife and

218

Para Bruin, the Rubber Bear

caught the body of Ali Dubh in a strong clasp. Next moment he had lifted him up and tossed him high into the air, as easily as he had tossed the Mifket. The Arab alighted in the top branches of a tall scarlet plant and clung to them in great fear lest he should fall to the ground and be killed. Indeed, so frightened was he that he uttered screams of terror with every breath, and forgot all about eating John Dough in the more important thought of how he might reach safety.

"Let's run!" exclaimed Chick, grasping John's hand. "Don't mind the Arab. If he falls it's good enough for him!"

"The Mifkets will rescue him, I'm sure," added the Princess. "See! there come some of the creatures now, with Black Ooboo at their head."

Hearing this, John hesitated no longer, but fled down another pathway with the children, and soon left the sound of Ali Dubh's cries far behind him.

Black Ooboo

That evening, when John came out of his tree house to watch the sunset, he found Pittypat, the white rabbit, sitting before his door.

"I've news for you, my friend," began the rabbit, in a grave voice. "Black Ooboo and the Arab who wanted to eat you have become fast friends, and together they are determined to destroy you."

"How did you know that the Arab wants to eat me?" asked John.

"I was hidden among the plants when you met, and heard your talk," replied the rabbit. "You must look out for Ooboo and the Arab, or they will surely do you a mischief, for the Mifkets now know that you are good to eat."

"It's kind of you to warn me," said John; but can you tell me of any way to escape from this island, good Pittypat?"

"Not just at present," returned the rabbit; "but our Prince is very wise indeed, and I will ask him what is best to be done. In the meantime you must keep away from your enemies as much as possible."

With these words the rabbit sprang into a low bush and disappeared, leaving John Dough to sad reflections upon his dangerous position in this lonely island.

Soon after daybreak next morning, while Chick and the Princess were out hunting berries for their breakfast, John went for a walk along the shore, and so engrossed did he become in his thoughts that he did not notice when a band of Mifkets stole upon him from behind and threw a coil of stout rope around his shoulders. Before he realized his misfortune he was bound fast with many turns of the rope. Then he found that he had fallen into the hands of his old enemy, Black Ooboo; but the Arab, to his great relief, was not with the party that had captured him.

Shouting with glee at the capture of the gingerbread man, the Mifkets led him away through the forest paths until they arrived at the clearing wherein the King lazily reclined upon his flat rock.

Ooboo at once awoke the aged ruler, who sat up and said in a weary tone:

"Have you taken the stranger prisoner, as I commanded?"

"We have," answered the black one.

John Dough was very indignant at the treatment he had received, so he addressed the King angrily, saying:

"By what right do you command me to be bound in this disgraceful manner? Did you not give me permission to live among you in peace?"

"I am a king, and the promises of kings should never be relied upon," said the old Mifket, winking slyly at his prisoner. "Since I first saw you the Arab has arrived, and he tells us that the material you are made of is very good to eat."

"Can the Arab understand your language?" asked John, in surprise.

"It seems so," answered the King. "In some parts of Arabia the people speak exactly as we do; so the Arabs are probably descended from our race. Anyhow, Ali Dubh understands us and we understand him, and we've decided to have a bite of you before he can eat you himself."

This was disturbing news to the gingerbread man, and he stood before the King wondering how

THE MIFKETS RECAPTURE JOHN

he might escape from this awkward situation when the black Mifket, who was squatting beside him, opened his mouth and bit off the thumb from John's left hand, which was tightly bound to his side.

"How does is taste, Ooboo?" inquired the King, while the black one was chewing the thumb.

"I can't exactly describe the flavor," said Ooboo, boldly biting off the forefinger of the hand.

John was enraged at this dreadful treatment, and his glass eyes had a dangerous flash in them. It didn't

224

pain him especially, for he had no nerves; but to be chewed up by a common forest Mifket was a liberty that any gingerbread man might well resent.

"Seems to me there's molasses in him," said Ooboo, with a wink at the King, and immediately he bit off another finger and ate it. "Also a bit of ginger," he continued, calmly, eating the next finger. "And spices." Another finger was gone. "It isn't exactly cake, and it isn't exactly bread," the black one proceeded, smacking his lips; "but it's pretty good, whatever it is"; and with that he ate the last finger remaining on John's left hand.

The King was no longer sleepy. He had become quite interested, and the circle of Mifkets that stood silently back of John were looking at their victim with hungry eyes.

"Bring him here to me," said the King. "I'll eat the other hand and see what it's like."

Ooboo immediately pushed the prisoner toward the rock; but John was now terribly frightened, and had made up his mind not to allow the rest of his body to be eaten without a struggle to save himself. So he suddenly exerted all the strength the Great Elixir had given him, and burst his rope bonds as easily as if they had been threads. At the same instant the Arab leaped into the group

225

that surrounded the throne and placed himself between the King and John Dough.

"Stop!" he screamed, his voice shrill with anger. "How dare you eat the gingerbread I have bought and paid for?"

"There's enough for all," said the King. "We'll divide him up, and have a feast."

"Not so!" shouted the Arab. "He's mine, and mine alone!"

But while they were thus quarreling the gingerbread man, free of his bonds, turned and fled swiftly into the forest, and before the Mifkets or Ali Dubh knew he had gone their intended victim was far away.

Chick was very indignant when John Dough entered the tree house and showed his mutilated hand.

"You ought to stay near me every minute," said the Cherub, "so I can take care of you and keep you from getting into trouble. If this thing keeps on, John Dough, you won't be able to present a respectable appearance."

"I know it," said John, sadly. "I'd escape in that little boat on the beach; only, if a rain-storm came up, there'd be no shelter and I'd become soaked and fall to pieces."

"HE'S MINE, AND MINE ALONE!"

227

"It is n't our boat, either," said Chick. "It belongs to the father and mother of the little Princess, and they may want to use it themselves, some day, to escape in."

"That's true," said John. "How is the Princess to-day?"

"She's worse," answered Chick. "Seems to me she gets weaker and more delicate every day."

"That's what the rubber bear says," John remarked, thoughtfully.

"See here," said the child, "that gingerbread of yours is full of strength and power, is n't it?"

"That's what Ali Dubh says," John responded. "The Elixir that I am mixed with is claimed to be very powerful."

"And it's true," declared Chick, "for I've seen you do things no gingerbread man could ever do without some magic Elixir being mixed up with him. Well, then, why don't you let the Princess eat the rest of your left hand, and get well? The hand is n't any use to you since Black Ooboo ate off the fingers."

John looked at his left hand nervously.

"What you say, Chick, appears to be true," said he; "but you've no idea how I dread to be eaten. I'm not very substantial at the best, and during my brief lifetime I've been crumbled and chipped and bitten to such an extent that I dread to lose even a crumb of my person more than is absolutely necessary. Of course I'd like to help the Princess, and restore her to health and strength; but perhaps we can find some better way to do that than to feed her on my gingerbread."

"Very well, John Dough," said the Cherub, getting up to go to the Princess, "I suppose you can do as you please about feeding yourself to your friends; but if *I* was gingerbread you can just bet I wouldn't be so stingy with myself!"

Left alone, John sighed and wondered if it was really his duty to sacrifice his left hand to save the frail little girl and restore her to strength and health. He wanted to be kind and generous, yet the very thought of being eaten filled him with horror.

Presently he left the tree house and wandered along the coast. Chick's rebuke disturbed him not a little, and he wanted time to think it over. So by and by, when he thought he was alone, he sat down upon a rock and tried to decide what to do. Suddenly a low rustle disturbed him, and he looked up to see the brown bear squatting beside him.

"Where's the Princess?" asked Para Bruin.

"Aren't you a good way from your mountain?" inquired John, instead of answering the question.

"Yes, I don't often stray so far," was the reply, "but I had an idea of calling on the Princess. Where is she?"

"She's sick to-day," said the gingerbread man.

"That's bad," declared the bear, shaking his head sadly. "She seems to be failing every day. Poor little Princess!"

John moved uneasily, for every word was a reproach to him.

"How are you getting on with the Mifkets?" asked Para Bruin.

"They made me a prisoner this morning, and abused me shamefully," said the gingerbread man. "See here!" and he held up the stump of his left hand.

"What has become of your fingers?"

"A black Mifket named Ooboo bit them off and ate them," was the answer.

"That's curious," said the bear, rubbing his nose thoughtfully with one paw. "Do you know, the Mifkets had an exciting time an hour ago? I watched them from my mountain, and saw everything. Black Ooboo had a fight with the King and knocked him off his rock. That's really surprising, for Ooboo has always before been a coward, and afraid of the King. But now he has declared he'll be king himself, and offers to fight any one who opposes him. Isn't that funny? I don't know where Black Ooboo got so much courage and strength all of a sudden, I'm sure."

"I know," said John. "He got it from my fingers, which he ate. My dough is mixed with the Great Elixir, you know, which is nothing less than concentrated energy and strength and vitality and knowledge. The fingers have made Ooboo the most powerful Mifket in the island, so it is no wonder he has become king."

Para Bruin listened to this carefully, and after a moment's thought he said:

"If that is the case, John Dough, you must feed some of yourself to the Princess to make her strong again."

"That's what Chick says; but I don't like to do it," said John.

"You will do it, though," said the bear; "for if you don't you are no friend of mine, or of any other honest person. I'm going back to my mountain, and if you don't save the little Princess I'll never speak to you again."

Black Ooboo

Away stalked Para Bruin, and John Dough arose with a sigh and walked far into the forest, trying to make up his mind what to do. He came to the bank of the brook presently, and seating himself upon a fence beside the stream gazed into the rushing water in deep thought. From the distance came the roar of water falling over the big dam which the beavers had built, and once or twice a Mifket strayed that way and looked curiously at the silent figure of the gingerbread man. But they had orders from the Arab and Ooboo not to

disturb him, so they crept away again and joined their fellows among the giant plants.

A long time John Dough sat there by the stream, until suddenly he was aroused from his musings by a shriek of discordant laughter behind him.

"Ho, ho, ho! What an absurd thing! Who'd ever have thought it?"

He turned around and saw a gorgeous macaw standing on a log back of him. The bird was all aglow with crimson and green feathers, and its black eyes twinkled mischievously, while continuous shouts of laughter came from its ruffled throat.

"Keep still, can't you?" said John, in an annoyed tone. "What are you laughing at, anyway?"

The bird pushed its head underneath a wing and shook with suppressed mirth.

"Oh dear! It's too funny for anything! What a lark—hoo, hoo, hoo! What a lark it is!"

Its voice was somewhat smothered by the feathers, but John heard every word, and it made him angry.

"You're a rampsy, that's what you are!" he cried.

233

Black Ooboo

"There are two of us—two of us—two of us!" shrieked the macaw, hopping around and fluttering its brilliant plumage. "Honestly, my dear breakfast, I never had so much fun in my life!"

John turned his head and looked at the bird earnestly.

"Why do you call me your 'dear breakfast'?" he asked, with sudden suspicion.

"Because that's what you are, my poor innocent! Ha, ha, ha! Breakfast is ready!" The bird made a quick thrust with its beak, and the next moment fluttered around in front of John with its mouth full of gingerbread.

Our hero quickly stood up and put his right hand behind him. The baker had made two little coat tails at the back of his waist, and as John felt for them he found that the thieving macaw had eaten both of these coat tails entirely off, while he had sat upon the log thinking.

"How stupid I am!" he exclaimed, with real grief. "I might have given those coat tails to the Princess, and now this silly bird has eaten them up!"

"I said you were a chump!" remarked the macaw, winking, and then laughing again. "The idea of your sitting there and letting me eat you! I never had so much fun in all my life."

Just then a great chattering reached his ears, and looking around, he found that a numerous band of the fierce Mifkets had stolen upon him, and were now coming forward armed with huge clubs which they had broken from the forest plants, and which were as solid and heavy as the branches of trees.

"Surrender!" cried the leader, knowing that the gingerbread man understood their language; "King Ooboo wants you for his luncheon, and Ali Dubh is also hungry."

For a moment John Dough was most frightened.

It was not likely that his strength would enable him to escape from so many of his enemies, and he almost gave himself up for lost. For before him was the stream of water — almost as deadly to him as the close ranks of the Mifkets behind him. The macaw was strutting up and down beside him, and at his look of despair the bird said:

"You're surely in a bad way, my friend; but I believe I can save you. When I fly up, grab my feet, and I'll carry you away to your dwelling."

"You!" he exclaimed, gazing at the bird in surprise; "you are by no means big enough to fly away with me."

"Size doesn't count for much," chuckled the macaw; "and since I breakfasted off your coat-tails I feel myself to be as strong as an ox. Just grab my legs, as I tell you to."

John decided that it was worth attempting, being the only thing to do. The Mifkets were pressing closer, and soon he would be within reach of their clubs. So, as the macaw flew into the air John grasped its legs with his right hand (which was the only hand that had fingers), and, sure enough, the strength of the little bird was so great that it easily drew him up into the air, high above the heads of his chattering and disappointed foes.

Black Ooboo

"Fooled again," cried the macaw; but of course the Mifkets did not understand the words. Away over the tops of the giant plants flew the bird, with John Dough clinging to its legs, and it was not long before it gradually descended again and landed the gingerbread man safely before the door of his own dwelling.

"Don't thank me," said the macaw, turning toward him one black eye, in a saucy manner, and winking comically. "I ate part of you for my breakfast, and feel greatly refreshed. Were it not for the Arab I'd hope to get another meal off you, but between the Arab and the Mifkets you're not likely to last long. Good bye."

And then it flew away into the forest.

Under Land and Water

Chick met him at the door.

"There's less of you than ever," said the child, looking him over carefully. "Your coat tails are gone now."

"Yes," said the gingerbread man, "a macaw ate them a few minutes ago. But there will be even less of me in another minute. Have you a knife, Chick?"

"What are you going to do?" asked the Cherub, with sudden interest.

"I'm going to save the Princess before I'm gone entirely," said John, with decision. "Not that I have overcome my dislike to being eaten, you understand, but if a black Mifket and a foolish bird find it so easy to feast upon my person, Ali Dubh is sure to get me in time, and before that happens I want to do one good deed, and help the little girl to regain her strength and health."

"Good!" exclaimed Chick, approvingly. "You're

all right, John Dough, even if it did take you a long time to make up your mind. But we have n't any knife."

"What shall we do?" John asked, anxiously.

"Can't we *break* off a chunk of you?" the Cherub inquired.

"No!" replied the man, with a shudder.

"Wait a minute!" cried Chick, "I've an idea."

Away trotted the chubby legs, and presently the child returned with a long, slender leaf, plucked from one of the strange forest plants.

"This'll saw gingerbread all right, I'm sure. Hold out your hand, John Dough!"

John turned away his head and held out his left hand—the one from which Black Ooboo had eaten the finger.

"There! It's all over. Did it hurt?" asked Chick.

"No." John looked at the arm where his hand had been.

"It is n't much worse than it was before," said the child. "You'll never miss it in the world. Now wait here while I go to the Princess."

After Chick had vanished into the girl's dwelling the gingerbread man gave a sigh of relief.

239

Under Land and Water

"It wasn't as bad as I feared," he said to himself; "but I'm glad the ordeal is over. If I take good care of myself hereafter, and manage to escape from Ali Dubh, I can get along very well without the gingerbread I have lost."

The Princess slept sweetly that night, after her supper of gingerbread, and the next morning was so fresh and bright, and had so pretty a color to her cheeks, that Chick hugged her delightedly, and John Dough was proud and glad to think his small sacrifice had wrought such good results. Together they strolled into the forest, along

the banks of the stream, and presently met Pittypat.

"Be careful where you go," said the rabbit, in a worried tone. "The Arab is after John Dough, and I hear that Black Ooboo has determined to destroy the little man with the red whiskers and the fat woman with the corkscrew curls, who are the father and mother of our Princess."

"Are you sure?" asked the girl, clasping her hands in real terror.

"There's no doubt of it," Pittypat replied. "And I'm not sure but the Princess will share their fate. These are troublous times, since the Arab arrived and Black Ooboo became king."

"There's the boat," said Chick, turning to the girl; "can't your parents escape in that?"

"They have always said they would use the boat to leave the island, if there was any danger," answered the Princess. "But the ocean is so big and the boat so very little that they did not like to make such a voyage unless it became necessary."

"Well, it seems to be necessary now," said John. "But what will become of the rest of us? The boat will only hold two."

"It might hold me as well as my parents, if the

water was calm," said the girl; "but I will not escape and leave you and Chick to your fate. Unless we can find some way to save us all I will let my parents escape alone in the boat."

"That's foolish," said Chick. "You go in the boat. John Dough and I will get along all right."

But this the Princess refused to do, and after a long discussion the rabbit decided to go and consult a gray owl which was renowned for its wisdom. The others walked up to Para Bruin's cave, and the first thing the bear said was:

"Look out for yourselves. Black Ooboo has ordered all the humans on this island to be killed, and the Mifkets are arming themselves with long sticks, to which they have bound sharp thorns torn from a tree in the forest. The gingerbread man is to be eaten, I understand; so there's likely to be an end of all of you, very soon."

"Is there no way to escape?" asked John.

"None that I can think of," said the bear. "But you can depend upon my assistance, if there is anything I can do. How well the Princess looks to-day!"

"Yes," answered John, proudly; "she's been eating some of my gingerbread."

Hearing this, Para Bruin gave John a grateful

hug; and then he hugged the Princess and even Chick, so happy did the bear feel at the girl's recovery.

Then he bounced for them several times, rolling himself down hill against the flat rock and then bounding high into the air. But the little Princess was worried and anxious about her parents, so the party soon bade good bye to Para Bruin and started to return to their dwellings.

The forest seemed very quiet and peaceful as they walked along, and they had almost forgotten their fears, when, just as they reached the banks of the brook, a sudden sound of shouting fell upon their ears, mingled with the wail of human voices.

"Oh, dear!" cried the little Princess, wringing her hands in great fear; "the Mifkets have attacked my dear parents, I am sure, and they will both be killed!"

John strove to comfort her, but he suspected that the Princess had guessed truly, and that her parents were in great danger. They dared not return to the seashore, for that would mean their own destruction; so they remained hidden in the forest, while the Princess sobbed as if her heart was broken, and John wiped away her tears with her handkerchief. He had one of his own;

but it was gingerbread, and would not stand the dampness.

Suddenly they heard pattering footfalls, and the white rabbit crouched at their feet. He was panting from a hard run, and his eyes were big and bright.

"They are gone!" said he, as soon as he could speak.

"Who are gone?" asked John, anxiously.

"The red-whiskered man and the woman with the corkscrew curls," replied Pittypat. "The Mifkets

chased them to the shore, but they jumped into the boat and rowed away in time to escape. The Mifkets threw sticks at them and Black Ooboo screamed with rage; but the father and mother of our Princess got away without being hurt in the least."

This good news greatly pleased the girl, and her anxiety was much relieved. But the ginger-bread man had become thoughtful, and asked Pittypat:

"What are the Mifkets doing now."

"They are getting ready to search the forest for you and Chick and the Princess," was the reply. "The Arab is with them."

"This is certainly unpleasant news," remarked the gingerbread man. "Did the gray owl tell you how we may escape?"

"The owl sent me to the King of the Fairy Beavers," replied the rabbit, "and he has consented to hide you in his palace. It is a rare favor, I assure you; but the Mifkets cannot reach you there."

"A Fairy Beaver!" cried Chick, gleefully; and the Princess asked, wonderingly: "Can a beaver be a fairy?"

"Why not?" inquired Pittypat. "All the animals have their fairies, just as you human folks do; and it is lucky for us that the Fairy Beaver lives on this very island. There is only one danger—that the Mifkets find you before I can lead you to the

Under Land and Water

Beaver King. So follow me at once, I implore you, before it is too late!"

He turned, with these words, and led them along the river bank at such a swift pace that the Princess could hardly keep up with him.

"How far is it?" asked John.

"The palace of the beavers is somewhere under the big dam in the river, which is not far away. The King promised to meet us at the waterfall; but he will not allow me to enter, because I am a rabbit, so you must go in alone. But have no fear. The King will allow nothing to harm you."

As Pittypat spoke they could hear the distant roar of the waterfall at the beavers' dam. But another sound also fell upon their ears — a sound that quickly renewed their terror — for it was the yells of the approaching Mifkets. Presently the fierce creatures appeared, coming swiftly through the forest.

"Hurry!" called Pittypat. "Hurry, or it will be too late!"

John picked up a great wooden club that lay near their path, and while Chick and the Princess hurried after the rabbit he stopped and hurled it toward the Mifkets. It fell among them with such force that several were knocked over and many

PARA BRUIN TO THE RESCUE

others howled with pain. It did not prevent them
from coming on, but they kept at a more respect-
ful distance from the gingerbread man, never
doubting they would be able to capture him in
time.

"This way!" cried the rabbit, leaping down the
bank to the side of the river, where they could
travel more swiftly.

The others followed, and now before them
appeared a wide and high sheet of water that fell
over the great dam that the beavers had built many
years before. They had almost reached it, and
Pittypat had called out that he saw the Beaver
King waiting behind the waterfall, when the fugitives stopped short with cries of despair. For just
before them appeared another band of Mifkets,
armed with the thorn sticks, and now they saw that
they would be unable to reach their place of
refuge.

John looked around in desperation. There were
Mifkets behind them and Mifkets before them;
and on one side was the deep river, and on the
other side a steep bank too high for the children
to climb. It really seemed to the gingerbread man
that they were lost, when suddenly a cry was heard,
and looking upward he saw Para Bruin standing

upon his high peak and watching them. The bear doubtless saw the danger of his friends, for he called to them:

"Look out — I'm coming to the rescue!" Then he quickly curled his great body into a monster ball and rolled swiftly down the side of the mountain that faced them.

The Mifkets who were near the waterfall turned curiously to watch the bear. They had often seen him roll against the flat stone and bound back to his place again, and thought he would do the same thing now. But old Para Bruin was more clever than they suspected. He missed the flat stone altogether and came bounding along at a

249

terrific speed. Before the group of Mifkets, who stood close together near the waterfall, knew what the bear meant to do, old Para's body shot upon them and dashed them in every direction. Some lay stunned upon the ground; but most of them were tumbled into the river, where they struggled frantically to regain the shore.

"Quick!" cried Pittypat, "your friend has saved you. But do not lose an instant's time!"

The children and the gingerbread man obeyed at once, and in a few steps reached the waterfall.

"Creep behind the sheet of water!" commanded the rabbit. "You will find the Beaver King awaiting you. Do as he tells you, and I promise that you will be safe."

"Good bye, Pittypat!" called the Princess, as she clung to the damp rocks behind the waterfall.

"Good bye!" echoed Chick. "Much obliged to you, Pittypat!"

"Good bye!" answered the white rabbit. "Don't forget me."

Then he whisked away, and John Dough, shrinking as far from the spray as possible, crept under the waterfall and followed after the little ones.

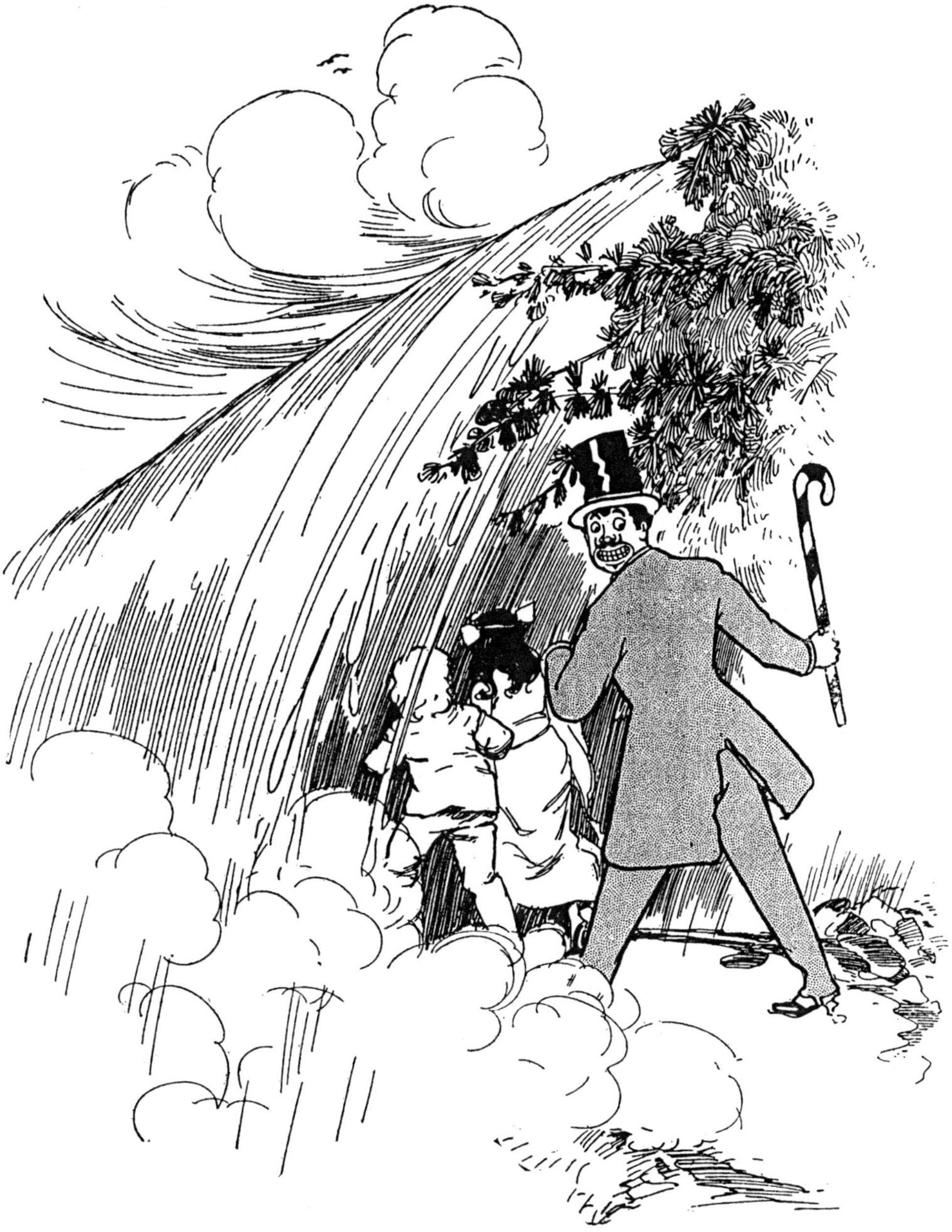

"CREEP BEHIND THE SHEET OF WATER"

The Fairy Beavers

The Mifkets uttered cries of rage as they observed the escape of their intended victims, and rushed forward to follow them. But immediately a great flood of water began falling just at the place where the children and John had entered, and as the Mifkets recoiled from this new danger our friends heard a soft voice say, with a little laugh:

"They will not dare to follow you now. Come with me, and be careful not to slip."

John looked down, and saw a handsome beaver standing beside him. His fur was the color of silver, and upon his head was a tiny golden crown set with jewels so bright and sparkling that the rays lighted the dim place like so many sunbeams. The Beaver King's face was calm and dignified, and his eyes kindly and intelligent. Without further speech he led the way far under the roaring waterfall; and the space between the dark wall of the dam and the sheet of water was so narrow that the air was filled with a fine spray, which moistened

252

The Fairy Beavers

John's gingerbread in a way that caused him great uneasiness.

But, lighted by the radiance of the King Beaver's crown, they soon came to a place directly under the center of the fall, and here their conductor halted and tapped three times upon the surface of the wall. It opened instantly, disclosing a broad passage, and through this the King led them, the wall closing just behind them as they entered.

The noise of the waterfall now sounded but dimly in their ears, and presently they emerged into a large vaulted room, which was so beautiful that the little Princess clasped her hands with a long-drawn sigh of delight, Chick laughed, and John removed from his head the crumpled and soiled silk hat that he had clung to ever since he had left the bakery.

He had seen beautiful rooms in the Island of Romance, but nothing there could compare with the magnificence and grandeur of this hall of the Fairy Beaver's palace. The walls were set thick with brilliant jewels, arranged in a way that formed exquisite pictures, all

of these borrowing color from the natural tints of the gems. The ceiling was clustered with tiny glass globes, in each of which was a captured sunbeam; and these lent a charming radiance to the splendid room. Many cushions were strewn upon the floor, and the floor itself was of gold, richly engraved with scenes depicting the lives and adventures of beavers.

While our friends admired the loveliness of the Hall of the Beavers, the silver-furred King spoke again, in his soft voice:

"You are now underneath the deep water formed by our dam, which was built by the beavers who were our forefathers many years ago, and which has endured until now. But in all the years of its existence the little Princess and the Incubator Baby are the first human beings to be admitted to our fairy palace. Your companion, my dears, is merely gingerbread, and lives by means of fairy powers that make him a fit comrade for fairies the world over."

"It was very good of you to save us from the Mifkets, and we are grateful," said the girl.

"You're all right!" added Chick, emphatically.

"I am glad to be of service to one so sweet and beautiful," returned the King, with a dignified bow toward the Princess, "and to one so merry and frank," he continued, turning to Chick. "And now, if you will kindly follow me, I will show you the rooms of my palace, and introduce you to my people. You must be content to remain my guests until I can find means to restore you to the freedom of the upper world in which you are accustomed to exist.

He led them through the gorgeous hall and along delightful passages into various rooms. Some were large and some were small, but all were extremely beautiful, and Chick wondered greatly at the extent of this under-water palace, the existence of which no one could suspect who stood in the forest above, beside the dam of the beavers.

"Are all beavers' homes like this?" asked the child.

"No, indeed!" answered the King, laughing softly. "They are usually houses composed of mud, mixed with bits of wood and the leaves and branches of trees. But I am King of the Beaver Fairies, who watch over the fortunes of all ordinary beavers and take care of them. We are invisible, even to beavers; and the eyes of mankind can never see us unless, as in your case, we permit them to do so. These rooms seem to you deserted, but

The Fairy Beavers

I assure you they are filled with many beaver fairies, who are even now watching you with much curiosity."

Both the children started at hearing this, and glanced hastily around; but nothing but the walls of the palace met their gaze, and the King smiled upon them indulgently.

"At our banquet, this evening," said he, "I will permit you to see my people. But now please come to the music-room, where you may enjoy the strains of harmony that provide us with one of our chief amusements."

He led the way to another room, the roof of which was dome-shaped. From different points in this dome projected the ends of many silver tubes, and near the floor of the room, directly underneath each of the tubes, was placed a plate of glass or of metal.

The King invited his guests to seat themselves, and then pressed a diamond button that was placed in the wall. This allowed the water from the river above them to drip slowly through the silver tubes; and as it fell, drop by drop, on the plates beneath, it made sounds that were very sweet and harmonious. The metal plates gave out deep and resonant sounds, while the smaller glass plates tinkled melodiously as the drops of water fell upon them.

Neither Chick nor the Princess recognized the first tune that was played, for it had been composed by one of the Fairy Beavers; but afterward the King played "Home, Sweet Home," for them, and "Annie Laurie"; and the music was so exquisitely sweet and soft that the girl declared she would never have imagined that sounds so delightful could be produced, and Chick pronounced the entertainment "all right."

The gingerbread man was also pleased; for it was the first real music he had ever heard, and it soothed and comforted him beyond measure.

The Fairy Beavers

The Fairy King seemed glad to give his new friends pleasure; and when the Princess remarked that she would like to know what the Mifkets thought of their sudden escape, the beaver led them to what he called the "Observation Room." In it was a square box, draped with black silk and having a window in one side.

Seating the girl and her companions before this window, the King said:

"You will now observe what the Mifkets are doing."

Instantly a picture appeared in the box, and it seemed that through the little window they were gazing upon a section of the forest they had recently left. There were the Mifkets, indeed, with Black Ooboo and the Arab among them, and all were quarreling and fighting among themselves in their usual way, and trying to decide what had become of the gingerbread man and the children.

"They are drowned and at the bottom of the river, by this time," Black Ooboo said; and his words came as distinctly to their ears as if they had been standing beside him.

"I hope not," answered Ali Dubh; "for I've never yet had a single bite of the gingerbread man, although I bought and paid for him."

IN THE "OBSERVATION ROOM"

The Fairy Beavers

Then the scene changed, and they saw Para Bruin climbing slowly up the side of the steep hill to his den. He seemed none the worse for his roll down the mountain and his bath in the river, and they noticed that he laughed and chuckled to himself as if much amused.

"That was a good fight," John Dough heard him murmur, in the bear language; "and I'm mighty glad I was in time to save the Princess, Chick, and the delicatessen man. They're safe enough with the beavers by this time, the white rabbit says!" Then he laughed again; and, reaching the top of the hill, entered his cave and lay down to rest.

Again the scene changed, and the Princess beheld the open sea, upon which floated the boat that bore safely her father and mother. They seemed to be quite comfortable, and the girl was pleased to see that they had put enough provisions and fresh water into the boat to last them during a long voyage. The man, although little, was strong, and pulled sturdily at the oars; and the woman steered the boat in the right direction.

Our Princess was very glad to see these sights, and to know Para Bruin was safe, and that her dear parents had escaped the fierce Mifkets. In company with her friend Chick and the gingerbread man, she wandered through the palace during all that afternoon, seeing many wonderful things that the Fairy Beavers had provided for the comfort and amusement of their community. It was, indeed, a little world by itself, placed under land and water, where no mortal could guess its existence.

In the early evening the King escorted them to a splendid banquet hall, where a long, low table was set in the center of the room. The dishes were all of sparkling cut-glass, and the eatables proved to be very delicious foods made from vegetables that grew at the bottom of the river, together with fish and lobsters and oysters, and many rare sweetmeats that could only have been created by the magic of the fairies themselves.

Around the long table were rows of silken cushions; but when the children and the gingerbread man entered, the room seemed deserted by all save themselves and the King.

His Majesty the King of the Fairy Beavers sat upon a cushion at the head of the table and graciously placed the Princess and Chick close to his right hand and John Dough at his left. Then he blew softly upon a silver whistle, and at once before the eyes of his guests appeared rows of

The Fairy Beavers

Fairy Beavers, occupying the cushions beside the low table.

They were all pretty to look upon, having silvery fur as soft as satin, and large dark eyes that

regarded the strangers pleasantly and without fear. From the neck of each was suspended, by means of silken cords, a richly embroidered cloak, exquisitely woven from a material unknown to the

262

The Fairy Beavers

Princess, and blazoned with an emblem denoting the rank or degree of the wearer. Also each of the Fairy Beavers wore a jeweled circlet upon the brow; but none of these was so magnificent as the diadem of their King.

While our friends gazed wonderingly upon the Fairy Beavers, the King introduced them, saying:

"This is a little mortal Princess named Jacquelin, whom I have protected because her heart is as fresh and innocent as the daisies that grow in the fields. This is Chick, known also as the Cherub, an Incubator Baby without relatives, but who is not lacking in friends. And this is John Dough, a strange creature, having the form of a man, made out of gingerbread. He is not exactly a fairy, but lives through the magic of a fairy compound known as the 'Great Elixir,' and is therefore not responsible for being alive and is liable to perish before he has grown very old. Each of these guests is, I believe, worthy of our friendship and protection, and I trust that my people will join me in welcoming them to our palace."

Answering the King's speech, all the Beaver Fairies gracefully arose from their cushions and bowed thrice—once to the Princess and once to Chick and once to John Dough. Then they all reseated themselves and drank to the health of their guests from dainty tumblers no bigger than harebells, which contained water as pure as crystal.

Then, while the feast began, a chorus of black beavers entered and chanted a pretty song; and afterward other beavers, so small that the Princess thought that they were quite young, entered and danced a minuet for the amusement of the entire company.

Chick and the Princess Jacquelin were really hungry, and although the children at first feared the food placed before them was not such as they could enjoy, they tasted some of the dishes and found them so delicious that both ended by eating heartily, and afterward decided they had never enjoyed a meal so much.

Of course John Dough missed the pleasure of eating, but he had a good time listening to the music and watching the dancers; so he was quite content. Later he amused the company by telling the story of his adventures since he had come to life in the bake-shop. He spoke in the beaver language, so that all understood him; and even the Princess could understand most of his speech, for the portion of gingerbread she had eaten had conveyed to her some share of the powers of the Great Elixir. The Fairy Beavers were much interested, and loudly applauded the recital.

After dinner the girl was escorted by six pretty Beaver Fairies to a cosy little room decorated with pink and white shells, which were polished smooth as glass. There was no regular bed in the room, but the beavers heaped many of the soft cushions into a corner, and upon these the Princess lay down and slept very peacefully until the next morning. Chick had a room of blue and gold, in the four corners of which perfumed fountains shot their sprays into the air. The tinkling sounds of these fountains might have soothed any child to sleep, yet Chick could have slept as soundly in the open forest as within this luxurious room.

John Dough also was supplied with a room in the palace; but as he did not sleep he had no need to lie down, and so amused himself during the night by looking at the beautiful pictures that decorated the walls and ceiling. Most of these depicted the work of beavers engaged in building dams and houses; John found them very interesting, and therefore passed a pleasant night.

Soon after daybreak the Beaver King came to John and escorted him to the Observation Room, where he found Chick and the Princess—who had already risen and finished their breakfasts—gazing earnestly through the window of the black box. He also approached the box to gaze at the shifting pictures, and discovered that the forest had become as quiet as usual, the Arab and Black Ooboo having returned to the village in the clearing, and only a few of the Mifkets being left to wander along the sides of the brook and watch the waterfall at the dam of the beavers.

"Now," said the Fairy Beaver to the girl, "I can do one more thing to please you. Make a wish, Princess, and I will grant it."

THE PRINCESS EMBARKS IN THE SUBMARINE

"Thank you!" she cried, eagerly. "I wish to rejoin my dear father and mother, wherever they may be."

"Very well," returned the King; "come with me."

He led them through many passages, until they reached a sort of tunnel that brought them to a rocky cave under the river bank, some distance below the waterfall. The water of the river covered half the floor of the cave, and upon the sandy beach at its edge rested a large glass cylinder, which was pointed at both ends and had a door in the top. Harnessed to one end of the glass tube were twenty-four strong beavers, who sat motionless beside it.

"The boat in which your father and mother are still riding is far out in the ocean," said the King to the Princess; "but in this submarine boat you will be drawn by my swimming beavers so swiftly that the journey will not seem long to you."

"Are we not to go with the Princess?" asked the gingerbread man.

"There is room for only one more in the boat," replied the King, "so the Cherub and you must bid farewell to your friend, in order that she may safely rejoin the parents she so dearly loves."

"I'm sorry," said John, sadly.

The Fairy Beavers

"I'm sorry, too," declared the little Princess. "for you have been very good to me, John Dough. Yet my parents need me more than you do, and it is my duty to rejoin them."

"That is true," said John. "Good bye, little friend, and may your life be long and happy."

Chick said nothing, but hugged the little girl in a long and warm embrace and kissed both her pretty cheeks.

The King now opened the door in the top of the cylinder and the girl stepped inside. The space was just big enough to permit her to lie down comfortably, and the bottom of the cylinder had been thickly covered with soft cushions brought from the palace.

The Fairy Beavers

When the King had closed and fastened the door, he gave a signal to the four-and-twenty beavers, and at once they dashed into the water, drawing the glass submarine after them, and began swimming with powerful strokes down the river. They swam well under the surface of the water, and the glass boat followed them without either touching the bottom or rising to the top.

At first the Princess was much bewildered by her strange journey, for it seemed as if the water was pressing upon her from all sides. But presently she realized that she was quite safe in the glass tube, and began watching curiously the pretty weeds and water-flowers that grew at the bottom of the river, and the queer fishes that swam around her.

The speed of the swimming beavers was surprising. It was not long, indeed, before they reached the mouth of the river and swam boldly out into the sea. Jacquelin had no idea of the direction they took, but she trusted to the wisdom of her friend the Fairy Beaver, and was not at all frightened.

And now the sights that she saw were very strange indeed; for the seaweeds were of most gorgeous hues, and there were not only big and little fishes of every description, but brillant sea-anemones and jelly-fish floating gracefully on all sides of her.

The journey was long, but not at all tiresome, and the girl had not realized how far she had been drawn through the waters of the ocean when a dark gray object appeared just overhead, and the beavers came to a halt.

Slowly the glass cylinder rose to the surface of the waves, and Jac saw just beside her the boat containing her parents. The girl's mother also saw, to her great surprise and joy, the form of her daughter lying in the glass case, and at once unfastened the door

271

and assisted the child to crawl out and scramble into the boat.

The first act of the little Princess was to kiss her father and mother delightedly, and then she leaned over the side of the boat and refastened the door of the cylinder.

"Tell your King that I thank him!" she called to the beavers, trying to speak their own language; and the intelligent little creatures must have understood, for the glass cylinder sank swiftly beneath the water, and she saw it no more.

Many days the Princess and her parents rode in the boat, until one morning they came to another small island and ventured to land upon it. They found it to be a beautiful place, inhabited by no savage beasts of any sort, and containing a grove of trees that bore figs and bananas and dates and many other delicious fruits.

So they built themselves a cottage on this island, and lived there in peace and happiness for many years.

The Flight of the Flamingoes

After the Princess had left them, John Dough said to the King: "What is to become of Chick and of me? We cannot stay with you always."

"I hardly know," answered the Beaver Fairy. "Is there any place you especially desire to visit?"

"No special place is known to me," said the gingerbread man.

"It doesn't matter where we go, so long as we keep going," added the practical Chick

"You have been very kind to us," continued John, "and we may rely upon your friendship. Since you possess such wonderful fairy powers, perhaps you will assist us to leave this island and get out into the world again, where we may seek new adventures."

"It shall be as you wish," promised the King. "But I must think of a way for you to leave my palace in perfect safety. Chick is in no great

273

danger, but should Black Ooboo or the terrible
Arab chance to capture you, they would cut your
gingerbread to bits in no time, and you would be
ruined.   For this reason it will be best for you to
leave this island as quickly as possible."

John readily agreed to this, and the King
remained silent for several minutes, engaged in
deep thought.   Then he said:

"I believe I know a way to save you, John
Dough.   But I must have your permission to cut
you into nine pieces."

"What good will I be when cut into pieces?"
asked John, somewhat alarmed at the suggestion.

"Do not fear," said the beaver.   "I promise to

274

The Flight of the Flamingoes

again restore you to your present form. The Mifkets have placed spies all about our dam, and if you attempted to walk away from here they would soon discover you. Therefore I will cut you into nine pieces, wrap each piece in a bit of cloth, and send the parcels by my beavers along different paths to the top of the hill where Para Bruin lives. There the bear and Chick can put you together again, for the child will have no trouble in reaching the bear's cave. After the nine parts are in place I will give you a magic cordial to drink; it will render your body as solid and substantial as it is now."

"But how can we escape from the island, once we have reached Para Bruin's cave?" asked John.

"The Flamingo people owe me many favors," answered the King. "You do not weigh much, so I will ask one of the flamingoes to fly with you to some other country. It will take two of the birds to carry Chick; but, if the child is not afraid, the journey will be perfectly safe."

"I'm not afraid," said Chick. "Anything suits me."

"I think your plan is an excellent one," declared John, "and we are both greatly obliged to your Majesty for your kindness."

The Flight of the Flamingoes

So the King brought a great knife, and with the assistance of Chick, who was much interested in the operation, cut John Dough into nine pieces. These were wrapped into packages and eight beavers were summoned, who carried eight of the packages through secret passages to the forest and then up the mountain-side to the cave of Para Bruin. The ninth package, containing the head of John Dough, the King undertook to carry himself, and although the Mifket spies of Black Ooboo noticed the nine beavers carrying packages up the hillside, they paid little attention to them, never suspecting that in this queer fashion the gingerbread man was making his escape.

And Chick walked boldly along the river bank and up the hill to meet Para Bruin, who hugged the

276

The Flight of the Flamingoes

child joyfully in his rubber arms, and tried to lick the plump cheeks with his pink rubber tongue. The Mifkets were puzzled by Chick's appearance, and wondered where the little one had come from; but they did not offer to interfere with the child in any way.

It was not long before the Beaver King reached the bear's cave and laid the ninth package, containing John's head, beside the other eight, which had already arrived.

"What's all this?" asked Para Bruin, eying the packages with much surprise.

"Be patient and you will see," replied the King, and then unwrapped John's head. When the bear saw it he uttered a groan and exclaimed:

"Alas! my poor friend has come to a sad end!"

"Not so," answered John's head. "The Fairy Beaver has cut me apart, but he has promised to put me together again, so that I will be as good as new. And you must assist us, friend Para."

"Most willingly!" declared the bear.

Then, under the King's direction, Para Bruin and Chick set up John's legs, and placed the sections of his body upon them, and afterward perched his head upon the body. John expected to tumble down at any moment, for he was just like a house of blocks that a child builds, and every one knows how easily that falls apart; but he kept as still as possible, and at length all the nine parts of him were in their proper places.

Then the King handed a small silver flask to the child, and told Chick to pour the contents into John's mouth — just between the candy teeth. Chick, by standing on tiptoe, was able to do this, and John drank the cordial to the last drop. He seemed to feel it penetrate and spread through all his gingerbread body; and, as it did so, every one of the cut places became solid again, and presently John took a step forward, looked himself over, and found he was indeed as good as new.

"That cordial is great stuff," he said to the King. "It's almost as powerful as the Great Elixir itself.

"It is an excellent remedy for cuts," replied the King, "and as you are so crumbly and unsubstantial I will give

The Flight of the Flamingoes

you anotner bottle of it, so that if you ever meet with an accident you may drink the cordial and recover." He handed John another silver flask containing the wonderful liquid, which John accepted with much gratitude.

"Now I must leave you," said the King. "The flamingoes have promised to send her their strongest flyers to bear you and the Incubator Baby to another land, so I believe you will both live to encounter many further adventures."

Chick and John again thanked the kind beaver for all the favors they had received, and then the King and his people returned to their beautiful palace, and left the gingerbread man and the cheerful Cherub and Para Bruin alone upon the mountain-top.

"What has become of the Princess?" asked the bear.

John told him the story of her escape, and Para said:

"Well, I'm glad the dear child was able to rejoin her parents; but this island will be a dreary place without her. I wish I could leave it as easily as you and Chick can."

"Perhaps," said John, "the flamingoes will also carry you."

The Flight of the Flamingoes

"Do you think so?" asked Para, eagerly.

"I'll ask them about it, for I understand their language," promised John; and this so delighted the rubber bear that he bounded up and down in glee.

Before long four great birds were seen approaching through the air, and soon they alighted upon the mountain close to where our friends stood.

"We were sent to carry a gingerbread man and a fair-haired child away from this island," said one of the birds, in a squeaky voice.

"I am the gingerbread man," replied John, speaking as the flamingoes did; "and here is the fair-haired child. But we also wish you to carry our friend Para Bruin with us. One of you can carry me, and two can carry Chick. That will leave the fourth to fly with Para Bruin, if you will kindly consent."

"What, that monstrous bear!" exclaimed one of the birds, indignantly.

"He's large, it is true," replied John; "but he's made of rubber, and is hollow inside; so he really does n't weight much more than I do."

"Well," said the flamingo, "if that is the case I do not object to carrying him."

John related this conversation to the bear, who

"NICE RIDE, ISN'T IT?"

The Flight of the Flamingoes

was overjoyed at the thought of getting away from the island.

A stout cord had been tied to the feet of each of the flamingoes, and John now proceeded to fasten the loose end of one of the cords around his own body, tying it in a firm knot, so it would not come undone and let him drop. The cords hanging from the two birds that were to carry the Cherub were tied together in a hard knot, and thus formed a swing in which the child sat quite comfortably. Para Bruin now tied himself to the fourth flamingo, and the preparations were complete.

"Are you ready?" asked the leader of the flamingoes.

"Yes," said John.

"Where do you wish to be taken?"

"We don't much care," replied the gingerbread man. "Let us get to some island where there are no Mifkets. As for Ali Dubh, he will be obliged to stay here with his friend Black Ooboo, and once I am away from these shores I shall be sure he can never eat me."

So the big birds flew into the air, carrying with them the gingerbread man and the fair-haired child and the rubber bear, and so swift was their

The Flight of the Flamingoes

flight that in a few moments the island of the Mifkets had vanished from their view.

"Nice ride, is n't it?" Chick called to John.

"Rather nice," answered the gingerbread man. "But this cord is so tight it's wearing a crease in my body."

"What a pity you are not made of rubber, as I am!" said the bear, cheerfully. "Nothing ever injures me in the least. I'm practically indestructible."

"How are you getting on, Chick?" asked John.

"Fine!" answered the Cherub. "This knocks Imar's flying-machine into a cocked hat."

Then for a time they sailed on in silence, dangling from the ends of their cords, while the strong wings of the flamingoes beat the air with regular strokes just above their heads.

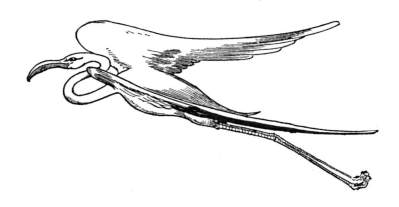

Sport of Pirate Island

The birds flew close together and made great speed, and in about three hours from the time they started an island appeared just ahead of them. Whereupon John said to the bird that bore him:

"Let us stop here, so we can examine the island and see how we like it. This cord is cutting into my gingerbread body, and I'd like to stop for a time, anyway."

"Very well," answered the bird; and when they were over the center of the island the flamingoes gradually descended and alighted upon the ground. John untied the cord from his waist, and also assisted Chick and Para Bruin to free themselves. The bear was not injured at all, but the cord had worn a straight line around John's body, although not very deep; and in some way the gingerbread man had lost another of his lozenge buttons.

The place where they had alighted was covered by grass and surrounded by groves of trees.

"This looks like a fine country," said Chick, gazing around.

Sport of Pirate Island

"It's better than our old island, anyway," remarked Para Bruin.

But just as he spoke the flamingoes uttered shrill screams and flew quickly into the air, and our friends turned in time to see a most curious creature come from the grove and approach them.

It had somewhat the likeness of a man, yet was too queer ever to be mistaken for a human being, although it was certainly alive. Its body was a huge punching-bag, and its head was a foot-ball. For legs it had two of those golf-clubs called "putters," and one of its arms was a tennis-racket and the other a base-ball club. This was curious enough, in all conscience; but the face was more curious yet. For the eyes were golf balls, and the nose a square of billiard-chalk, and its mouth a mere slit in the foot-ball where the lacing

had come undone. Taken altogether, this odd creature presented a most surprising appearance, and while John Dough and Para Bruin stared at it in amazement Chick boldly asked:

"Who are you?"

"Sport is my name, and sport my nature," answered the creature, winking one eye frightfully, and grinning until its queer mouth curled up at both corners of the slit.

"Sport," remarked the rubber bear, gravely, "is something amusing; so I am sure you are misnamed."

"Oh! you're a balloon," returned Sport, kicking at the bear with one of his golf-club feet; "the kid's a chucklehead and the other's a bun."

"I'm not a bun!" exclaimed John, indignantly.

"Yes, you are! Cross bun, too. Hot cross bun. Cool off, old chap, and look pleasant."

John was too angry to reply to this speech, but Chick said to the creature:

"If you're going to be so disagreeable, you'd better leave us. We don't care to associate with people of your sort."

"Ho, ho! ha, ha!" laughed Sport; "don't care to associate, eh? Do you know where you are?"

"No," said Chick, "and I don't care."

THE RETIRED PIRATES

Sport of Pirate Island

"Well, this island is inhabited by retired pirates and bandits, who make every one that lands here pay a heavy ransom, or else —"

"Or else what?" asked John, as Sport stopped short and gave another horrid wink.

"Or else they boil 'em in oil for three days," was the reply.

"Well," said the bear, "we can't pay a ransom, that's certain; but I'm not afraid of being boiled in oil. I'm practically indestructible."

"But I'm not!" cried John, much alarmed. "It would ruin my gingerbread to be boiled in oil, and Chick would certainly get overheated. I'm afraid it would melt your rubber, too, my dear Para."

"Would it?" asked the bear, with a start. "Then let us get away from this island at once!"

"By all means!" agreed John Dough.

"And the sooner the better," declared Chick.

But as they turned to look for the flamingoes, the creature who called himself Sport began pounding his punching-bag body with his tennis-racket arm, and at the sound a crowd of men ran out of groves of trees and quickly surrounded the rubber bear and Chick and the gingerbread man.

These men had heavy beards, hooked noses, and

288

piercing black eyes; and they wore red sashes tied around their waists; and laced leggings, and blue flannel shirts open at the throats; and in their belts were stuck many daggers and knives and pistols.

"Whoop! whoo—o—o!" they screeched, yelling like Indians; and their leader, who was uglier looking than any of his followers, cried out:

"Avast, there, my hearties! Here's a chance for either a fine ransom or a pot of boiling oil!"

"Then it's the oil," said Para Bruin, despondently; "for we have no ransom."

"You may as well start the bonfire," remarked Chick.

But John Dough stepped up to the pirate chief and asked:

"How much ransom do you require?"

"Well," answered the chief, "you're not worth much, yourself, and the child's too small to count; but a fine rubber bear like that is worth ten pieces-of-eight or a sparkling jewel."

"I will give you a sparkling jewel for him, as a ransom," said John, "provided you will then permit us to depart in peace."

"All right," agreed the pirate; "hand over the sparkler and you may go."

So John borrowed a dagger from the chief and picked out of his body one of the three diamonds which the inventor had given him in the Isle of Phreex. It glittered most beautifully in the sunlight, and the eyes of the pirate also glittered with greed. For he had noticed two other scars on

John's gingerbread body, similar to the one the diamond had been picked out of. Taking the diamond in his dirty hand he said:

"Well, where are the other jewels?"

"You agreed to accept this one as our ransom," answered the gingerbread man.

"You misunderstood me. I said three," declared the pirate; and turning to his men he shouted: "Didn't I say three, boys?"

"You did! You said three sparklers!" cried the retired pirates and bandits, in a loud chorus. So John, with a sigh of regret, picked the other two diamonds out of his body and gave them to the chief.

"Now," said the pirate, "I will allow you to go. But where you can go to is a mystery to me, for you are on an island."

"Stop!" cried another man, as they turned to depart. "You've got to settle with me, now. I'm the bandit chief, and I also demand a ransom."

"I have given the pirate chief all the diamonds I had," said John.

"Then you shall surely boil in oil!" shouted the bandit, scowling fearfully. "Seize them, my men, and away with them to the fiery furnace."

But just then came a flutter of wings, and the four flamingoes flew down and sailed along just over the heads of the prisoners. Instantly the bear clutched the end of a cord and was drawn upward by one of the birds. John Dough grasped the foot of another flamingo with his right hand, and was also raised high above the heads of the astonished pirates and bandits, while Chick coolly sat within the loop of string dangling from the two remaining birds and sailed into the sky with admirable grace.

Meantime the robbers shook their fists and yelled at the escaped prisoners in a frenzy of helpless rage.

"Wait a minute!" Para Bruin called to the flamingo which was carrying him; for he observed that just beneath him was the form of the dreadful person who had called himself Sport. The bird obeyed, remaining poised in the air; and at once the bear curled himself into a ball, let go the cord, and fell downward toward the ground.

The ball of rubber, rapidly descending, struck the surprised Sport and smashed him flat upon the ground. Then up into the air bounded the bear again, and caught once more the cord that was attached to the flamingo's foot.

"Well done!" called the Cherub, while the pirates and bandits were rushing to assist the helpless Sport.

"That was a noble deed, my good Para!" said the gingerbread man.

"Oh, I'm a bouncer, all right!" answered the bear, proudly. "But now let us get away from this awful place as soon as possible."

So the flamingoes flew swiftly across the sea with them, and John Dough found that he sailed more easily while clutching the bird's foot than when the cord had been fastened around his body. Chick also rode with perfect comfort, but Para Bruin was obliged to wrap the cord several times around his fat paw, to prevent it from slipping out of his grasp.

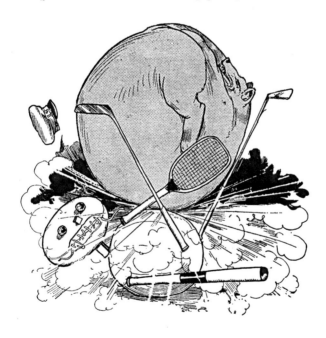

Hiland and Loland

After a long and steady flight the birds reached another island, larger than the first, and much more beautiful. The adventurers looked down upon green valleys and vine-covered hills, patches of stately forest and fields of waving grain. But aside from the scattered farm-houses, they saw no cities or villages until they were over the exact center of the island, where a most curious sight met their view.

The island was divided into two halves by a high and strong wall of stone, that ran from ocean to ocean, passing exactly through the center of the land. In the middle of the island the dividing wall was broken by a great castle, which looked upon both sides of the wall, and had many imposing towers and turrets and spires stretching high into the air. Clustered near to the castle and upon the east side of the wall were many tall and narrow buildings, some of them rising to a height of three or four stories. The windows in these buildings were tall and narrow, and the doors were tall and narrow, and the chimneys were

THE CASTLE OF HILAND AND LOLAND

tall and narrow. It was quite a city in size, but the houses all looked as if they were set upon stilts, while the streets were also narrow.

On the west side of the wall, adjoining the castle, was also a city, but of a quite different sort. For the houses were low, none being of more than one story, and the windows and doors in them were so broad and low that they were wider than they were high. As for the streets, they were remarkably broad. The cities upon both sides of the wall were pretty and well built, and there were many beautiful parks and pleasure grounds scattered about.

Our friends had not much time to observe these things closely, for at John's request the flamingoes alighted upon the top of the great wall, near to an entrance of the castle.

"We must leave you now," said one of the birds, "for we are obliged to hurry home again. But I am sure you will be quite safe in this beautiful country."

"Good-by," said John, "and thank you very much for bringing us here."

Chick and the bear also thanked the kind flamingoes, and then the birds flew into the air and soon disappeared.

Hiland and Loland

"What a lovely place to bounce!" said Para Bruin, leaning over the edge of the wall nearest to the tall houses and gazing downward into the street.

"It's a good way down," said Chick. "You'd better be careful."

"Nonsense!" replied the bear, scornfully. "The higher the wall the finer the bounce."

With that he made a ball of himself and rolled off the wall. John and Chick leaned over and saw the rubber bear strike the pavement far below and then bound upward again. When he was on a level with the top of the walls he reached out his paws, caught the edge of the stones, and drew himself up beside them.

"Great,—wasn't it?" he asked, proudly.

"Yes; but I advise you to be careful," said the gingerbread man. "We know nothing of the people who inhabit this country, and if you should chance to miss the wall when you bound upwards you would become a prisoner and be at the mercy of those who captured you."

"That's true," agreed the bear. "I'll be more careful until we get better acquainted. What shall we do now?"

"Let's try to find a way into the castle," suggested Chick. "It's the only way to get off this wall, for I can't bounce as you do, Para Bruin."

"Nor can I," added John. "How strange it is that the island should be divided by this great wall! And how queer to have everything short on one side and tall on the other! But perhaps the people in the castle can explain it all."

They walked along the broad wall toward the castle, and presently came to the large entrance gate, one of the wickets of which stood ajar, as if inviting them to enter.

"Shall we go in?" asked John, hesitating.

"Of course," decided Chick, promptly. "What's the use of staying outside, when the door's open?"

So they passed through the wicket and entered a lofty arched hall, built of blocks of exquisite marble, that gave it a grand and majestic appearance. There was a small stairway leading upward and a large stairway descending to the lower floors of the castle; but no one was in sight to greet them, so they decided to go down the stairs.

"Evidently they did not expect us," remarked Para Bruin.

"This must be the castle of the ruler, or king," replied John, "and perhaps the royal family is at dinner, or the king is holding court."

But at the foot of the stairs they found the hallways and rooms as deserted and empty as could be, and their footsteps echoed with a hollow sound upon the tiled floors.

The furniture of the castle was magnificent beyond description, and the draperies and pictures upon the walls were of exceptional beauty. Everything was in perfect order, yet the place seemed wholly deserted.

After inspecting the rooms on this floor of the castle they found another stairway, built of polished white marble, with elaborately carved marble balustrades. This they also descended, and discovered that the rooms on the lower floor were even more splendid than those they had already seen.

Occupying the entire central portion of the castle

was a great marble hall, having a domed ceiling, and windows which looked upon the tall city to the east of the wall, as well as upon the low city to the west. There were also great entrance doors, admitting people from both sides of the wall; but these doors were closed.

They were not locked, however, and John said to his companions: "We know nothing of the owner of this castle, nor of the people inhabiting the opposite sides of the great wall. They may prove to be either our enemies or our friends, so I advise that we be cautious until we know what treatment we may expect from them. Two of us should remain here while the third boldly enters inot the cities to make inquiries."

"I'll go," said Chick.

"No, indeed; you're too young and too small," objected Para Bruin.

"But I'm just a regular child, while you're a rubber bear and John Dough's a gingerbread man," said the Cherub. "They wouldn't think anything of my being here; but if either of you two go there's liable to be trouble."

"The Cherub is wise for one so young," observed John. "Therefore we will let the child visit the cities and report to us. Having found the castle

"THE CHERUB IS WISE FOR ONE SO YOUNG"

deserted, we will take the liberty of occupying it until our little friend returns."

So they opened one of the great doors, and Chick walked boldly out into the main street of the high and narrow city to the eastward.

Pacing before the entrance, as if guarding the doorway from without, was a soldier who stood more than seven feet in height, but who was so exceedingly thin and slender that it really seemed as if some strange power had stretched him out lengthwise. But Chick noticed that all the people walking along the streets of this city were just as tall and slight as the soldier, and quickly understood why the doors and windows of their houses had been built so singularly tall and narrow.

The soldier seemed surprised when the Cherub emerged from the deserted castle, but he took off his tall hat and bowed politely. His uniform was of blue cloth, with brass buttons.

"What place is this?" asked Chick.

"This, beauteous stranger, is the great country of Hiland," answered the soldier, respectfully. "And this is the great city of Hie which you see before you; and the great people you observe are called Hilanders; and I do not suppose there is so

302

great and wonderful a country, or city, or people anywhere else in all the world."

"What is the castle called?" asked the child.

"We call it the castle of Hilo," said the man. "It was the dwelling of the former King of Hilo, who ruled over our great nation as well as over the miserable creatures residing on the other side of the wall."

"But where is your King now?" inquired Chick. "The castle is empty."

"To be sure the castle is vacant at present, for our King is long since dead," the soldier replied. "But we are patiently awaiting the arrival of his successor. There is a prophecy that our next ruler will be a King who is wise and just, but not made of flesh and blood, and although this seems an impossible thing, our people hope that the prophecy will some day be fulfilled."

"But why don't you make one of your own people king?" asked Chick.

"Because the island is divided into two sections, and one king must rule both sides of the wall," replied the man. "Of course we would not allow one of the insignificant Loes to rule us, nor will they consent to allow one of our noble Hies to rule them. Therefore we must get along without a king until the arrival of the wise and just ruler who is neither flesh nor blood."

"Who are the Loes?" the child asked.

"I have never seen them, my dear, for the great wall divides them from our superior nation," said the soldier; "but they are said to be short and squat, and very disagreeable. They live on the other side of the island."

"Thank you for the information," said Chick, and then turned and re-entered the castle.

"What did you find out?" inquired John and Para Bruin, in the same breath.

The child carefully related the conversation with the Hie soldier, and then said:

"Now, I'll go into the other city, and find out what the people on that side of the wall have to say."

So John and Para opened the door at the opposite side of the arched hall, and the Cherub passed out and came upon another soldier, who seemed to be standing guard at the castle entrance. This one was dressed in a red uniform, with silver buttons, and was the shortest and fattest person Chick had ever beheld. But his broad face was smiling and

good-natured in expression, and he tipped his low, flat hat gracefully to the pretty Incubator Baby.

"What country is this?" asked the child.

"This, most lovely one, is the superb and grand country of Loland," replied the man; "and this splendid city you behold is the city of Lo; and our magnificent people are called Lolanders."

"What is the castle called?" Chick inquired, curiously.

"It is the Castle of Lohi, inhabited by our King —when we have one— who also rules the poor barbarians who dwell outside of our paradise, on the other side of the wall."

"When do you expect to have another king?" asked the Cherub.

"Whenever one comes who is wise and just, and is not made of flesh and blood," replied the man. "We have a legend that such a king shall rule us, but for my part I do not believe there is a person of that description in all the world."

"Yet there may be," suggested Chick, who had been thinking that the description just fitted John Dough.

"Oh, of course there may be," agreed the man, cordially; "and if there is, and he comes to our island, every one on both sides the wall will hail him as king."

Looking along the streets of the city of Lo, Chick saw that all the people were as short and fat as this soldier, and that they waddled like ducks when they walked. But they seemed as busy as bees in a hive, and appeared to be happy and contented; so the child could not decide which was the finest country—that of the short people or that of the tall ones. Both cities seemed prosperous, and on both sides of the wall the island was charmingly beautiful.

It may appear strange to the reader that neither of the soldiers Chick had spoken with made any attempt to question the child. But afterward our friends found that one of the established laws of the island forbade any of the people to ask questions either of strangers or of those inhabiting the country on the opposite side of the wall. However, they were not forbidden to answer any questions properly addressed to them, and by nature both the tall people and the short people were extremely courteous and polite.

Chick decided this queer law was to blame for the misunderstanding between the two nations, for, as neither country knew anything at all about the other one, a feeling of mutual contempt and indifference had arisen between them.

King Dough and his Court

After the conversation with the soldier, Chick went back to the hall of the castle and told John Dough and Para Bruin what the man had said.

"They all expect a wise and just ruler, who is not made of flesh and blood," reported the little one; "so I guess it's up to you, John, to run this island."

"I'm surprised," said Para Bruin, "that they do not prefer a king who is made of pure rubber and can bounce. But if they want John Dough instead of me I'm willing to yield in his favor."

"You shall be my Chief Counselor," replied John; "only I reserve the right to act as I please in case I do not like your counsels."

"That is entirely fair and reasonable," declared Para Bruin, "and I thank you for the honor you have conferred upon me."

"I'm going to be Head Booleywag," said Chick, gravely.

308

King Dough and His Court

"What's that?" asked John.

"It's the one that rules the ruler," said the smiling Cherub. "So just behave yourselves — you and your Chief Counselor — and you'll both find I know my business."

Thereupon the child led John Dough to the King's attiring-room, and hunted in the closets until a fine ermine robe and a crown and scepter were discovered. The crown was a little tarnished

309

King Dough and His Court

from lack of use, but the jewels in it still sparkled brightly; so the bear set it upon John's gingerbread head and put the scepter in his right hand. Chick folded the ermine robe around him in such a way that his missing left hand was not noticed, and then they led the gingerbread man to the great hall and placed him in the royal throne.

He might have looked more dignified had not his nose been badly chipped and his left glass eye so loose in its socket that it rolled every way but the right way; however, the robe concealed the fact that his shirt-front was soiled and cracked, and that several lozenge-buttons had broken off during his recent adventures. But kingly robes and a kingly crown cover many defects, and when Para Bruin and the Cherub stood back and took a critical look at their friend they felt quite proud of his regal appearance.

When all had been made ready and John was seated in the throne, Chick went to the west door of the castle hall and threw it open, and at the same time Para Bruin opened wide the east door. Then, together, they cried out to the people:

"The King has come! Enter his castle, all ye Hilanders and Lolanders, and greet the new ruler in a fitting manner!"

KING DOUGH THE FIRST 311

King Dough and His Court

So the tall and slender people trooped in at one door and the short and fat people trooped in at the other; and all gazed with awe and reverence at the strange form of the gingerbread king, who was surely not flesh and blood, and might easily be a wise and just ruler.

There was no disputing the fulfillment of the prophecy; so all bowed humbly before John, whom Chick introduced to his subjects in a shrill, childish voice as "King Dough the First, ruler of the Twin Kingdoms of Hiland and Loland."

Afterward there was feasting and rejoicing in both cities, and John made a royal procession on both sides of the great wall, being everywhere received with shouts of enthusiastic joy.

The gingerbread man proved a very successful ruler; and as neither he nor Para Bruin ate anything and Chick returned to a diet of oatmeal and cream, the King's expenses were very light, and he was not obliged to tax his people to support his royal state.

One of the first laws he made was that no one in the two nations should eat gingerbread that was more than three days old, under pain of death; this prevented his ever being in danger when he traveled in either land.

Another thing he did was to engage a fat little woman of Loland to make and bake him a new gingerbread hand, having five excellent fingers at the end of it. Also she made gingerbread patches

to fit his broken ear and his crumbled nose and his
damaged heel, as well as some lovely new coat-
tails; and when the hand and all these patches
were placed where they belonged, John drank the
cordial contained in the silver flask that the Beaver
Fairy had given him, and at once the new gingerbread became a part of his body, and he was as
perfect as the day he had left Monsieur Jules'
bake-shop.

The woman also repaired his frosting and
fastened some new lozenge-buttons to his waistcoat, after which John presented so neat and
respectable an appearance that all his people were
very proud of him.

Para Bruin also became a great favorite in the
two cities, and the tall and short folks loved
to watch him stand upon the high wall that
divided the two nations, from which he would
leap to the ground and immediately bound back
again to his station on the wall. He was always
good-natured and cheerful, quite winning the
hearts of the Hilanders by poking fun at the
Lolanders, and afterward delighting the Lolanders
by jeering at the Hilanders.

So Para Bruin's life was a happy one, and for
countless years he remained the close friend and

King Dough and His Court

companion of King Dough the First, the popular and worthy ruler of Hiland and Loland.

The Records of the Kingdom say very little of Chick's later history, merely mentioning the fact that the King's most valuable assistant was the Head Booleywag, who grew up to be the especial favorite of all the inhabitants of the island. But, curiously enough, the Records fail to state whether the Head Booleywag was a man or a woman.

THE END

Printed in the United States
111199LV00003BC/85-130/P